THE ADVENTUROUS FOUR AGAIN

D1428511

This Armada book belongs to:

_____

_____

_____

THE
ADVENTUROUS
FOUR AGAIN

Enid Blyton

Armada

First published in the U.K. in 1947
by George Newnes. This edition was first
published in 1962 by William Collins Sons & Co. Ltd.,
14 St. James's Place, London SW1A 1PF

This impression 1977

© Enid Blyton 1947

Printed in Great Britain by
Love & Malcomson Ltd.,
Brighton Road, Redhill, Surrey.

Back with Andy Again

THREE very excited children bumped along a rough country lane in a farmer's cart. The Scottish carter sat in front, saying nothing, but listening with a little smile to the children's happy voices.

"We shall see Andy again soon! We haven't seen him since our exciting adventures last summer!" said Tom, a red-haired boy of twelve.

"It was bad luck getting measles in the Christmas hols. so that we couldn't come up here and stay in our little cottage," said Jill. She and her sister Mary were twins, and were very like each other. They each had long golden plaits and blue eyes, and were younger than Tom.

Tom spoke to the carter. "Jock! Did you hear about our adventures last year?" he asked.

Jock nodded his head. He hardly ever said a word.

The children, with their friend Andy, had indeed had some thrilling adventures. They had gone out in Andy's father's fishing-boat one day, and had been caught by a storm. They had been swept miles out of their course on to a lonely island—and had found a nest of enemy submarines in the waters there, hiding to pounce on any ships that came within their reach.

"And poor Andy lost his father's boat," said Jill, remembering how afraid Andy had been of what his father might say about the lost boat.

"But it didn't matter—because Andy was given a much, much better boat!" said Mary. "And it was called *Andy*—do you remember, it had his name painted on it? Wasn't Andy pleased?"

The fisher-boy had been more than pleased. He had been filled with the greatest delight. The new fishing boat was a magnificent one, with a lovely red sail. Andy's father had been overjoyed too, for a fishing-boat meant his livelihood to him. Catching fish and selling them was his work and Andy's—and now they had one of the finest boats on the coast.

The farm-cart jolted along, and soon the children came in sight of the sea. The coast there was rocky and dangerous, but the sea was a lovely blue, and the children shouted in joy to see it.

"The sea! There it is! And look—there are the fishing-boats out on it!"

"I bet I can see Andy's," shouted Tom. "Look—that one with the bright red sail! Isn't that Andy's, Jock?"

Jock nodded, and the three children fixed their eyes on the red-sailed boat. Andy's boat! Andy was out there on the restless sea—and soon they would go out with him. What fun they would have!

Their mother was already waiting for them in the cottage she had bought in the fishing village. She had gone there two days ahead of the children to get things ready for them, when they broke up from school. It was the Easter holiday, and everywhere the trees were leafing, the hedges were greening, and the banks were starred with primroses, violets and celandines.

"A whole month's holiday by the sea—with Andy and his boat!" said Tom. "I simply can't think of anything lovelier. I don't expect we'll have any adventures *this* time —but that won't matter."

"We had enough last summer to last us for years," said Jill. "I was frightened sometimes—but it all ended happily."

"Except for those hidden enemy submarines!" said Tom. "They didn't have a very happy ending! Look—there's Mother!"

Sure enough, it was their mother, standing at the next corner, waving. The children tumbled out of the cart and flung themselves on her.

"Mother! It's lovely to see you. Is everything all right?"

"Is the cottage ready? Have you seen Andy?"

"I'm awfully hungry, Mother. Is there anything nice to eat?" That was Tom, of course. He was always hungry. His mother laughed.

"Welcome back to our little village, children! Yes, there's plenty to eat, Tom. And yes, I've seen Andy. He was sorry he couldn't meet you, but there's a good shoal of fish in, and he had to go out to help his father in the boat."

"Does the boat go well?" asked Tom eagerly. "It was marvellous last summer. I've often thought of Andy whilst we were at school, and envied him. There he was, sailing out in all weathers, having a wonderful time—and I was writing Latin exercises at school, and being ticked off because I threw a rubber at someone."

"Oh Tom—don't tell me your report is a bad one!" said his mother, as they all walked down a slope to the little fishing village below. Jock came behind carrying large trunks as easily as if they were empty boxes!

"When will Andy be back?" asked Jill. "Has he changed, Mother? Is he still the same old Andy?"

"Of course," said her mother. "He's grown a bit taller —and a bit broader—but he's almost fifteen now, you know. You're nearly thirteen, Tom! You've grown too. So have the girls. You'll see Andy later in the evening, when the fishing-boats come back. He promised to come straight up and see you."

"We'll go down to the shore and wait for his boat to come in," said Tom. "After we've had something to eat, I mean. What is there, Mother?"

"Ham, eggs, three kinds of scones, two kinds of jam, and a fish-pie," said his mother. "Will that do for you?"

"I should think so," said Tom, who felt as if he could eat the whole lot at once. "Golly, it's good to be back again, Mother—and to think of all the sailing we'll have!"

"Well—don't find enemy submarines this time," said his mother, as she swung open a little white gate that led through a tiny garden to the cottage. "I really couldn't bear it if you got lost on a lonely island again."

They all ran up the path to the wooden door. It stood open. A bright fire burned in the living-room, and the table was set with so many dishes of food that Tom gave a whoop of delight.

"Golly! Must I wash my hands? Can't we begin now?"

"No. Wash first," said his mother firmly. "You all look like sweeps. Would you like boiled eggs to begin with, or fish-pie?"

"Both!" shouted Tom, and ran to wash in the little sink that was the only place where water ran from a tap.

They all made an enormous meal. "I can see I shall have my work cut out to satisfy your appetites these holidays!" said their mother. "No—you needn't help to clear away and wash up, twins. I've got Mrs. MacIntyre coming in to help. You can put on your jerseys and shorts and go down to meet Andy. I expect the boats will be putting in soon, if they've made a good catch."

The children hurriedly pulled off their school-clothes, and scrambled to find their jerseys and shorts. The weather was fine and sunny, almost like summer. If only it would stay like that all the holidays!

They raced down to the shore. Fine, soft sand lay between the rocks that jutted up all over the beach. A little stone jetty ran a short distance into the water. To this jetty the fishing-boats came with their hauls.

Andy's boat was clearly to be seen, a good way out. But now they were all coming in—the *Sea-Gull*, the *Mary-Ann*, the *Jessie*, the *Andy*, the *Starfish* and the rest. The breeze filled the sails, and they billowed out prettily.

"It's a fine sight, a fishing-fleet coming home!" said Tom, running up the jetty and down, so excited that he couldn't stand still. "I wish I had a boat of my own! Hi, Andy, Andy! Come in first, show us what your boat can do!"

Almost as if Andy had heard, the red-sailed boat surged forward in front of the others. The wind swept down on her, and she glided along like a red-winged bird on the water.

"There's Andy! There's his father too!" shouted Jill. "Andy, we're here! Have you made a good catch?"

"Ahoy there!" came Andy's voice. "Ahoy!"

Then the beautiful boat came deftly to the stone jetty, and Andy leapt off. He and Tom shook hands, both grinning widely in delight. The twins flung themselves on the fisher-boy and hugged him, squealing in delight.

"Andy, you've grown! Andy, you're browner than ever! Oh, Andy, we're all back again, isn't it lovely?"

"Grand," said Andy, as pleased as they were. He repeated the word and rolled the *r* in it even more. "Gr-r-r-r-rand!"

Then his father jumped out to make the boat fast. He smiled at the three children, and shook hands gravely with them all. He never had much to say, and the children knew he was strict with Andy, and made him work hard. But they liked him and trusted him.

"You'll help with the fish, Andy," he said, and the boy

8

turned at once to bring in the great catch they had made. The children helped too.

"I do think the beginning bit of a holiday is lovely," said Mary. "I think I like it best of all."

"Yes. The middle and end parts slip away so quickly," said Jill. "But you sort of feel the beginning bit will last for ever!"

"Can we go sailing with you soon?" asked Tom. "This evening, Andy?"

"No—not to-day," said Andy, knowing that his father would not let his boat out again. "To-morrow perhaps, if we're allowed. Dad may not want the boat to-morrow. We've had such a good catch to-day."

"Is it nice to see your own name painted on your boat?" said Mary. "*A-N-D-Y*—doesn't it look lovely?"

"It's your boat as well," said Andy. "I always told you you could share it when you were here. It ought to be called the *Andy-Tom-Jill-and-Mary*!"

All the other boats came in. The children greeted the fishermen. They knew them all, and they knew the fine little fishing-boats that bobbed gently up and down beside the jetty. But they felt that Andy's boat—their own boat —was the very best of all!

"It's getting dark," said Tom, with a sigh. "We'd better go home. We promised Mother we'd be in before dark —and golly, I do feel tired. We've had a jolly long journey to-day, and we'll feel better to-morrow. I just feel now I want one thing—to fall into bed and sleep!"

"What—don't you want any supper!" said Jill. "You *must* be tired, Tom!"

Andy laughed. He was happy to see the twins again and to have his friend Tom. Four whole weeks together! They would have some fun.

"See you to-morrow," said Andy, as the three said good-bye and turned away from the shore. "I'll be along."

Back they went to the cottage, all feeling suddenly tired. They could hardly eat any supper—and then they undressed quickly, washed, and fell into their beds, half-asleep before their heads touched the pillow.

"To-morrow—lots of tomorrows!" said Jill, but Mary didn't answer. She was asleep and dreaming of all the exciting to-morrows.

Off on a Sailing Trip

THE next few days were lovely. Andy took them sailing in his boat, which he insisted belonged to them all—a quarter each.

"I'll have the red sail for *my* quarter," said Jill. "I do love it so! Andy, can't we go out with the rest of the boats, when they go fishing?"

"Oh yes," said Andy, and out they went the next time the little fleet went out. Andy taught the children how to let down the nets. They watched with excitement the jumping, slithering, silvery fish, caught in the meshes of the great net.

The fisher-boy taught them how to set lobster-pots, too, in the right places. They took home enough fish and lobsters, scallops and crabs to keep them in food for a week!

The sun shone. They grew brown. They climbed the rocky cliffs all about, and had a wonderful time. Then Tom grew restless and wanted to go off on a longer trip.

"Let's go somewhere exciting," he said. "Can't we take the *Andy* and go on a trip somewhere? Don't you know anywhere thrilling, Andy, you could take us to?"

"Well," said Andy, "I promised your mother I wouldn't take you right out to sea any more, to visit any of our islands—in case a storm came up, like last year, and wrecked us. So it would have to be somewhere along the coast."

"Do think of somewhere," begged the twins. "Somewhere that nobody goes to."

"There's the Cliff of Birds," said Andy suddenly. The others stared at him.

"The Cliff of Birds," said Jill. "What a funny name!"

"It's a good name." said Andy. "There are thousands of birds there—I couldn't tell you how many—all kinds!

Gulls, shags, cormorants, puffins—they nest there and all round and about—on the cliffs, in the cliffs, over the cliffs —everywhere. They say you can't walk a step this season of the year without treading on a nesting-bird. They're a sight to see."

All the three children were fond of birds. Their eyes shone.

"Let's go there!" said Tom. "What a sight it would be! I'll take my camera. We're having a snap-shot competition at my school next term, and I could enter some bird pictures for it."

"Yes, do let's go," said Jill. "It sounds exciting. I wonder you never told us about the Cliff of Birds before, Andy!"

"Well, last time you were here, it was full summer," said Andy. "The birds have left their nesting-places on the cliffs by then, and are out on the open sea. There's not much to see. But at nesting-time it's different. They're all there."

"Well, we'll go," said Tom. "How far is it? Can we get there and back in a day?"

"We'll have to," said Jill. "Mother won't let us go off for a night, I'm sure!"

"If we start early in the morning we'd be back before dark," said Andy. "It's a long way—and it's a lonely part of the coast too. We'll have to be careful, because there are rocks all about. But there's a passage between them that my father knows. I'll get him to tell me. I've been twice with him."

"When shall we go?" asked Jill, beginning to feel excited. "To-morrow?"

"No. I'm wanted on the boat with my father," said Andy. "But maybe the next day. You'll have to do without me to-morrow. You get out your book on birds and read it well, then you'll know the birds on the cliff when you see them."

So, all the next day, the children pored over their books on birds, looking up each sea-bird, studying it, and learning its name. Tom got out his camera and put a new roll of films into it. They told their mother where they were going.

"It certainly sounds exciting," she said. "I hope Andy knows the way down the coast well. It's rather dangerous round here."

11

"Oh, Mother, Andy could sail a boat anywhere!" said Tom. "He's been twice before, anyway. Won't it be exciting to go somewhere that nobody ever goes to?"

"The Cliff of Birds," said Mary. "Thousands of them, Mother. You'll see them if Tom gets some good snaps. I suppose we shall climb the cliff."

"I'd better have a word with Andy about that," said her mother, and she did. But Andy assured her that he wouldn't let anyone do anything they couldn't do safely and easily.

Two days later the children awoke with a jump, as the alarm clock went off. It had been set for dawn—how early it was! Tom slipped into the girls' room to make sure they were awake, and not going off to sleep again.

"The sky's just turning silvery in the east," he said. "Hurry up. We've got to be at the jetty in a few minutes. I bet Andy's already there."

Their mother appeared in her dressing-gown, looking sleepy. "I thought I would just see you off," she said. "Now, you do promise to be careful, don't you? Andy's got life-belts on board, hasn't he?"

"Oh, Mother, you know we can all swim like fish!" said Jill.

"Yes—in calm or slightly rough water," said her mother. "But if you fell overboard in stormy waters you'd find things much more difficult. You've packed the food on board, haven't you?"

"Oh yes," said Tom, who could always be trusted to look after the food side. "We put it on board yesterday evening—everything you gave us, Mother. It will last us nicely for a day."

"It would last most families for a week!" said his mother. "Now—are you ready? Take woollen coats with you, because it isn't summer, you know. Tom, where's your mack?"

Soon they were off. The sky was much lighter now. The children could see golden fingers coming up from the east. The sun was just below the rim of the world there. They raced down to the jetty, feeling the wind quite cold on their faces and their bare legs.

Andy was there, of course, waiting for them patiently. He grinned when he saw their excited faces. "Get on board," he said. "Everything's ready. I'll cast off."

The children tumbled on board the fishing-boat they loved. It was roomy, but not too big for them to handle. It had a small, cosy cabin below. All three children were good at helping Andy now, and could be trusted with anything.

The boat slid away from the jetty. The breeze billowed out the red sail. Then, quite suddenly it seemed, the sun appeared above the sky-line, a dazzling rounded edge, and at once the water flashed with golden lines and twinkled brilliantly as the boat plunged forward.

"The sun's rising," said Jill, and caught her breath at the sudden beauty of it all. "The world's all new again. Look at the sun—it seems to be climbing out of the sea itself!"

Soon the children could no longer look at the sun, it was so big and bright. The boat went slipping along in waves that seemed made of golden light and blue shadows. It was worth coming out so early just to see the enchanting beauty of the rising sun.

"Heaps of people have never seen the sun rise," said Jill, as she leaned over the side of the boat to look at the gold-flecked waves. "Hardly any of the girls at my school have. They've missed something! I think there ought to be a law that says everyone must watch a sunrise, and everyone must see a bluebell wood, and a buttercup field, and . . ."

"Look out for the sail!" yelled Andy, as the big red sail swung across. Jill ducked, and forgot what she was saying. Andy was at the tiller, looking browner than ever. His dark hair blew straight upright in the wind, and his eyes shone as blue as the sea.

"I say," began Tom, "isn't it about time to . . ."

Everyone interrupted him. "To . . . have something to eat!" they all chanted, knowing Tom's ways very well indeed.

"I wasn't going to say that," said Tom, aggrieved. "I was going to say—oughtn't we to keep closer to the shore now? We're heading right out to sea."

"Got to," said Andy, keeping a firm hold on the tiller, as the boat swept into a strong current "There are rocks farther in. Can't risk them in this boat. We must keep out a fair bit, then, when I see the spot my father told me of, I'll swing inland a bit."

13

Andy had a rough chart with him. He pushed it across to Tom, holding on to it till the boy had it safely, because of the rushing wind.

"Look at that," he said. "Those dots are rocks. See how the sea nearer in is peppered with them. Sly rocks they are—just below the surface. They'll scratch a hole in the bottom of a boat in the twinkling of an eye. It takes us longer to go out to sea, and then turn in, but it's safer. We've got to look out for three tall pine-trees on a cliff, before we turn in. They're marked on the map."

Everyone studied the map with interest. What a long way down the coast the Cliff of Birds was! No wonder Andy said they must start early.

"What time shall we be there?" said Mary.

"We should be there about eleven, with luck," said Andy. "Maybe before. We'll have our dinner then. We'll be hungry!"

Tom looked really alarmed. "What! Are we to wait till then? We'll be starved!"

"Oh, we'll have breakfast first," said Andy. "We'll have it at seven, or half-past. Maybe a few biscuits now would be nice. What do you say, girls?"

Everyone thought it was a very good idea. "Biscuits *and* chocolate!" said Jill. "They go so well together. I'll get them."

She disappeared into the little cabin below, and came back again with four rations of biscuits and chocolate. Everyone was soon munching, Andy still at the tiller. He said he was not going to let anyone else steer the boat that day, it was too dangerous!

The sun was much higher in the sky now. It was warmer, though the strong sea-breeze was cold. Everyone was glad of woollen jerseys, cardigans and macks on top.

"Now—here's where we head inland," said Andy suddenly. "See those three pine-trees on the cliff, far away over there?"

"You've got eyes like a hawk, Andy," said Tom, screwing his up to try to see the pine-trees on the distant coast. He could just make them out. But neither of the girls could see them clearly.

Andy swung the boat round a little. The sail flapped hard. The boat now ran even more quickly, and the child-

14

ren felt thrilled with the speed, and the up-and-down swing of the fine little boat.

"Breakfast-time!" said Andy. "We're doing very well—we deserve a jolly good breakfast!"

"We *do*!" said Tom, and scurried to get the food.

The Cliff of Birds

BREAKFAST was a very welcome meal. There were hard-boiled eggs, scones and butter and a tin of peaches. Jill heated some milk down in the little cabin and made cocoa, which they all enjoyed.

Now the boat was heading shore-wards, and the rocky cliffs could be clearly seen. It was about eight o'clock. The sun was higher in the sky, and its warmth was very welcome.

"My word—what a lonely, desolate coast!" said Tom, watching it as the boat sped along. "And look at those wicked rocks, Andy, nearer the shore."

"Yes—there are some out here too, so we've got to keep a look-out," said Andy. "The worst are marked on that chart. I know them all. In about an hour's time we have to slip between an opening in a rocky ridge we'll come to, and skim along in a kind of channel between two rows of rocks. We're all right if we get into the channel. It's like a sea pathway, and so long as we keep in the middle of it, we're all right."

At about nine o'clock the children saw ahead of them a very turbulent stretch of water. The waves frothed and surged and sent spray high into the air.

"Look out!" said Tom, pointing ahead. "There must be rocks there."

"Yes—just about here is the opening I told you of," said Andy. "We've got to slip through it as soon as we come to it. I think it lies beyond that big surge of water."

He cleverly skirted the bubbling, frothing patch, where the waves were torn into shreds on rocks that hardly showed above the surface. Then the children gave a shout.

"Here's the entrance—look—a nice, calm little bit!"

Andy steered the boat deftly through the little passage, the opening through the outer ridge of rocks. The boat careered along, its sails full of wind, and slid into a channel between the outer and inner rows of rocks. Fairly calm water ran there.

"There are horrid rocks on each side of us," said Jill. "But here we're safe! How far does this queer calm channel go, Andy?"

"It flows to Smuggler's Rock," said Andy, "but we swing landwards before we get there, to the Cliff of Birds."

"Smuggler's Rock! What an exciting name!" said Tom, and he looked at the map. "Oh yes—your father's put it in—at least, I suppose this dot, with S.R. beside it, means Smuggler's Rock?"

"That's right," said Andy. "We've a good way to go still. My, aren't these lonely waters? We haven't sighted a ship on the sea or seen a soul on land since we left our village behind!"

"It's a wild bit of the coast," said Tom. "I wonder why Smuggler's Rock was given that name, Andy? Were there smugglers there in the old days?"

"I don't know," said Andy. "I've only seen the Rock from the distance. It's like a small steep island made entirely of rock. Nothing grows there, I should think—except seaweed round the foot. Maybe there are caves there that smugglers hid things in. I don't know anything about it. Nobody goes there now—and maybe they never did! Maybe it's just a name."

"It's half-past ten," said Tom, after a time. "Shall we soon be there, Andy—at the Cliff of Birds?"

"Why, are you getting hungry again?" asked Andy, with a grin.

"Well—I am," said Tom, "but I wasn't thinking of that. I was thinking of the time, and how long we'd have there. We'll have to allow a good many hours for getting back."

"We'll have a couple of hours at the Cliffs and no more," said Andy. "But it will be enough. You'll be able to climb up the cliff and explore it a bit, and have some dinner, and maybe take some photographs. Then we'll have to go back."

"Is that Smuggler's Rock, look, right over there!" suddenly shouted Jill, pointing westwards. The others looked, and saw a small, rocky island rising above the waves a fair distance away. Almost at the same moment Andy swung the boat to the left, and headed for the shore.

"Yes—that's Smuggler's Rock," he said. "And did you

17

notice that the channel we were in went on towards it? But I've swung away now, because we're coming to the Cliff of Birds. See the birds on the water now, and flying above it!"

As they sailed nearer to the Cliff of Birds the children shouted in amazement at the amount of birds to be seen everywhere. Gulls called, and the sound of their laughing voices, which Jill said reminded her of the mewing of cats, echoed all round them. Birds bobbed up and down on the water, skimmed the waves, soared high and low in the air.

"Now, when we round this rocky point, you'll see we come into a kind of shallow bay, and the cliffs behind are the ones I've brought you to see," said Andy. "They are covered with the kind of little narrow ledges that sea-birds love for their nests. They must have used the cliff for hundreds of years."

The *Andy* rounded the point, and then swept into a shallow bay. The children gazed at the towering cliffs behind, too astonished to speak.

There were birds there by the thousand! They lined every ledge, they called from every point. They launched themselves from the steep cliffs into the air, and soared and glided on the currents of air, crying and calling at the tops of their wild voices.

The sight of the red-sailed ship startled them. A hundred or so flew up from the cliffs, and their flight startled hundreds more, so that the rushing of wings sounded like a mighty wind. Tom gave a cry.

"What's that falling down the cliff—look, it's like a rain of white drops tumbling down!"

"Eggs!" said Andy. "These sea-birds lay their eggs on the bare ledges of rock, you know—and they are jolly careless with them. When they fly off suddenly they often make their precious eggs roll off—then down they fall and smash on the rocks below."

"What a waste," said Jill. "I wish we hadn't frightened them. But what a sight, Andy! I've never, never, in all my life seen or heard so many birds together before!"

"Andy, look—there's a river rushing out at the bottom of the cliff," said Tom, excited. "*Is* it a river? It seems to be coming out of a cave! Right out of the depths of the cliff."

"Yes, it's a river," said Andy, bringing the boat in gently. "It must flow right through the cliff. And look—do you see that waterfall splashing half-way down the cliff? That comes out of a hole somewhere up there. I suppose it couldn't find a way to seep down through the rock, so it has forced itself out up there, and made a waterfall."

"It's a very exciting place," said Jill. "I wish the birds wouldn't make quite so much noise, though. I can hardly hear myself speak!"

"Where are we going to put the boat?" asked Mary. "There's no jetty—and no sand to drag her on to. What shall we do?"

"I'll guide her into the deep pool under that overhanging cliff," said Andy. "And let down the anchor. She'll be all right there. We can jump across to the rocks nearby."

"Let's have dinner first," said Jill.

"Well—only just a snack now," said Tom, to everyone's surprise. "I'm longing to explore that bird-cliff. It's marvellous, really marvellous. We don't want to waste too much time eating. If we had a snack now, we could make a good meal on the way back."

"Right," said Andy. So they hurriedly made some sandwiches of bread and butter and potted meat. They ate them, had a drink, and then, with the *Andy* lying quietly at anchor, looked to see which rock would be the best to jump to.

"There's a rock just under water here," said Jill, peering over the side of the boat. "We'll tread on that, and then we can easily get to that big rock there, and so to the rocky ledge at the bottom of the cliff."

They took off their shoes and tied them round their necks. Then they made their way across the rocks to the foot of the cliff. Not far off the river that came out of a cavern in the cliff surged into the sea, frothing and seething where its current met the waves of the sea. The waters there boiled and surged and made a great noise. Altogether it was a very deafening place, for the sea-birds never once stopped their loud clamouring and calling.

"I'll find the easiest path up the cliff," said Andy, who was as good as a goat on hill or cliff. "You follow me carefully. It's a steep cliff, but not dangerous to anyone like us that's used to climbing about. Look out for any slippery

19

"Oh, Andy, it makes me feel so giddy," said Jill

bit. You go last, Tom, in case one of the girls should slip."

With the clamour of the birds round them, and a ceaseless swish of wings, the four children began their steep climb. There were plenty of good footholds and handholds, but their parents would certainly not have liked to watch them going slowly upwards, higher and higher. Soon they looked like specks against the towering cliffs.

They had their rubber shoes on again now, and Tom carried his camera slung over his shoulder. Soon they came to the nesting-places, high up beyond the reach of any stormy waves. The frightened, angry birds flew off their eggs. There were no nests at all. Jill was grieved to see yet more eggs roll into the sea.

"Some of them don't fall off," she called. "They just roll round and round. Look what a funny shape they are—awfully pointed at one end."

"Eggs shaped like that don't roll away so easily," said Andy. "They are meant to roll round and round in exactly the same spot."

Soon they came to a narrow ledge that seemed almost like a pathway round the cliff-side. It was about halfway up. Jill suddenly gave a cry.

"Andy! I've just looked down! And oh, I don't like it a bit! I might fall, it makes me giddy."

"Don't be silly," said Andy, who didn't mind heights at all. "You've never minded before. Follow me, and I'll take you round the cliff a bit, where there's a wider place you can rest in. You're tired!"

Trembling, poor Jill followed Andy closely, not daring to look down at the far-away sea again. Neither Tom nor Mary minded a bit. They thought it was funny of Jill to feel afraid.

The ledge was a favourite nesting-place for the birds, and the children had to be careful not to tread on the eggs. Jill was glad when the rocky pathway widened out, and became a fine resting-place. At the back of this resting-place was a shallow cave. The children crawled into it, and lay there, panting, warm with their climb.

"I'll just go out and see if I can take a few snaps," said Tom, at last. But just as he was about to go, he stopped. He heard a noise that sounded most peculiar in that deserted, sea-bird-haunted place—the sound of somebody whistling a well-known tune! How very strange!

A Real Puzzle

THE whistle sounded loud and clear. The children listened in the utmost astonishment. Somebody on the Cliff of Birds! Who in the wide world could it be?

A wild clamouring of sea-birds began again and the whistling was drowned in the noise. The children looked at one another.

"Did you hear that?" said Tom. "It was someone whistling!"

"We'll see who it was," said Andy, and he half-started up. Jill pulled him back.

"He might be cross if he knew we were here. He might be a bird-watcher or photographer or something—and if he thought we had disturbed the birds, he'd be angry."

"Well—it's our cliff as much as his," said Andy, shaking his shoulder free from Jill's hold. The whistling sounded again, very clear indeed, and a scraping sound told the children that the whistler must be coming near.

"He's just above us!" said Jill, in a startled whisper. "Oh—look!"

Above the cave they were resting in, was a narrow ledge. On this ledge the whistler had sat himself down, for, dangling over the top edge of the cave suddenly appeared a pair of bare legs.

The children stared at these legs in silence. They didn't like them a bit. They were enormous legs, and on the end of them were enormous feet, very dirty indeed. The legs were covered with thick black hairs, almost like the fur of an animal.

Somehow the children felt that the owner of these legs would be as horrid as his dangling feet! They didn't say a word. Jill's heart beat rather fast. She stared at the swinging feet, and wished they would go away.

The whistling went on and on. Then, dropped deliberately down to the rocky ledge that lay in front of the cave, came some sea-birds' eggs. They were flung down to make a splash as they smashed. The children felt indignant. How horrid of anyone to break birds' eggs on purpose like that!

But no one said a word. There was something about those great legs that made them feel rather afraid. Whoever was up there didn't know there was anyone about but himself—and he would be the kind of fellow who wouldn't welcome children at all! Whatever could he be? Not a fisherman, surely.

And how could he have come to the Cliff of Birds? The children had seen no boat in the bay below. They hoped that the man wouldn't spot their boat, either. At the moment they felt sure it couldn't be seen from where the man sat.

"Let's wriggle right to the back of the cave," whispered Tom. "In case that fellow comes down a bit lower and sees us."

They wriggled back. They could still see the dangling legs, with their big ugly feet and toes. Then they saw something else. The man was swinging a pair of field-glasses by their strap, and the children could see them going to and fro by the man's feet.

The whistling stopped. "Twelve o'clock. Noon," said a growling voice. The glasses were swung up again, and the children wondered if the man was using them. What was he looking for? Something out to sea?

There was a low exclamation. Clearly the man had seen what he was looking for. The children strained their eyes into the distance, trying to see if any ship was on the horizon—but they could see nothing at all.

After a while the man got up. His horrid legs were drawn up one by one and disappeared. Thank goodness! The children imagined that a man with such enormous legs must be almost a giant!

There came a scrambling noise and a few bits and pieces fell from the ledge above the cave as the man walked off. The whistling sounded again, but stopped after a little. Then there was silence.

Andy crawled out of the shallow cave and listened cautiously. Nothing to be heard. He went out on to the wide ledge and peered up. He came back to the children.

"Not a thing to be seen," he said. "I say, you know, it's a bit of a puzzle—how did that man get here?"

"He must have come overland if he hasn't got a boat," said Tom. Andy shook his head.

"No. There's no way overland at all. Never has been. Sometimes bird-men have come to this cliff to study the sea-birds, but they always had to come by boat. The cliff is unclimbable the other side, and very dangerous."

"Well, but Andy—he must have come by boat then!" said Tom.

"Then where has he hidden his boat?" said Andy. "We couldn't help seeing it down there in the water, if it had been there, could we? It's impossible to hide a boat in this shallow bay."

"Where's he gone now?" asked Jill. "Up the cliff-path?"

"He must have," said Andy. "But I always thought the path stopped not far above where we are. Perhaps there's a cave where he's living. I've a good mind to go and see!"

"No, don't," said Jill. "I didn't like the look of his legs at all. I'm sure he is a huge, ugly, hairy kind of man—like a big gorilla, or something!"

"Silly!" said Tom. "He may be quite nice. Though I must say I don't feel as if he is, somehow! Nasty growly sort of voice he had too."

"Well—I'm going to see if I can find out where he's gone," said Andy, getting up. "After all, even if he sees me, what does it matter? Anyone can come here and watch the birds."

"I'll come too," said Tom. "I've had enough of resting. You two girls stay here. We won't be long."

The girls wanted a little more rest after their long climb, and were quite content to be left. They lay back, and listened to the sound of the boys climbing up to the ledge above the cave entrance.

"The ledge makes a kind of narrow path here again," they heard Tom say. "Come on—this is the way that man must have gone!"

The boys climbed up the rocky path. They were glad the girls hadn't come, for in places it was very narrow— nothing but a goat-path, Andy said. There were no goats though, in that part of the country, for there was not enough for even a goat to eat! Very little grew on that rocky cliff, except for a hardy cushion of sea-pinks here and there.

As they rounded a corner of the cliff, they heard a rushing sound. "The waterfall," said Andy. "It must come out of the cliff just near here. As far as I remember it quite bars the way."

They saw the waterfall the next moment. It was a magnificent sight, though the waterfall was not a very big one. But the sight of the torrent of water suddenly flinging itself out of the cliff, making a slight arch in the air and then falling headlong down the steep rocky cliff, gleaming and glittering as it went, made the two boys stop in wonder.

"I wish the girls could see this," said Tom. "Let's go back and get them."

"There's not time," said Andy. "Tom, it's queer we haven't spotted that man yet, isn't it? There's been no place he could hide in at all on our way here. Not even a place where a rabbit could hide. Where's he gone?"

"Beyond the waterfall, of course!" said Tom.

"He couldn't go beyond," said Andy. "Can't you see how the water completely bars the way? Who could get through that terrific gush? He'd be swept down the cliff with the torrent!"

The boys were now beside the waterfall. It fell down the cliff with a clamour as loud as the gulls made. It almost deafened them, and they had to raise their voices to speak to one another.

Tom gazed at the water gushing out from the hole in the cliff. He imagined it rushing through the dark, silent heart of that towering cliff, hidden away in narrow channels and tunnels—to come out suddenly into the sunshine, and leap downwards in joy, to join the sparkling sea below.

He felt puzzled. Certainly it was very strange to think that the man whose legs they had seen was nowhere about! Had he fallen off the cliff? Horrid thought!

"Do you think he's fallen off?" said Tom. Andy shook his head.

"No. He must be used to these cliffs, or he wouldn't be on them. He's somewhere here."

"Well, *where*?" demanded Tom, feeling quite exasperated. "We haven't overtaken him—and you say no one could get across this waterfall without being jerked down the cliff with it—and you don't think he's fallen down the cliff! Then where is he!"

"I don't know," said Andy, frowning. He looked to see if there was a way above the waterfall, but the rocky cliff there was smooth and steep. No one could climb over the waterfall that way. He bent down and looked under the water, that formed an arch as it jerked itself from the cliff.

"No. It would be too dangerous to try and creep under that," he said. "And anyway there doesn't seem to be any ledge the other side. Golly, it's a puzzle!"

They turned to go back, quite baffled. As they made their way along the ledge the noise of the waterfall suddenly seemed to lessen. The boys looked back.

"The torrent isn't so strong," said Tom. "There's less water coming out, look."

"I expect it varies," said Andy. "Sometimes I suppose it's a great gush of water, other times it slackens, and there wouldn't be much waterfall to see."

"Yes. I bet after a heavy rainfall the waterfall gets enormous," said Andy. "And in a very dry spell in summer there would hardly be any water coming out at all. It just depends on how much rain we've had."

"It's funny—the waterfall has almost stopped now," said Tom. "Just a trickle coming out! I wonder why."

"Come on," said Andy, getting impatient. "The girls will be wondering what's become of us."

They rounded a corner, and made their way back to the girls, who were now waiting impatiently for them.

"Not a sign of that man," said Tom, to their great astonishment. "He's simply vanished into thin air! Queer, isn't it?"

"Yes," said the twins in surprise, and demanded to know everything about the waterfall, and what it was like.

"We'll tell you when we get back to the boat," said Andy. "It's getting a bit late, and we ought to be starting. Also I'm hungry for my dinner. We only had a snack, you know."

They all started down—and when they had gone just a little way, they heard a sound that once more gave them a surprise.

"That whistle again!" said Andy. "Well, the man *is* somewhere about then! Where in the world does he hide? How I'd like to know!"

A Good Trip Back

IT was certainly astonishing to hear the man whistling again, when they felt certain that he wasn't anywhere near!

Andy stopped and looked back, but he could see nothing. "We can't go back and have another look," he said. "We haven't time. Golly, *where* could the man have been, Tom, when we went all the way to the waterfall?"

"It beats me," said Tom. "But never mind—we'll give it up! I want my dinner much more than I want to go and find out where that man hid!"

So down they went and down. It was much easier to go down than up. Jill was sensible and did not look at the sea at all this time, in case she felt giddy again. After a time they all stood safely on the rock at the bottom of the cliff. Not far off was the underground river, sliding turbulently out of the cavern at the foot of the cliff.

Soon they were in their boat again. It was bobbing gently on the pool where they had anchored it. They clambered aboard, and the girls went down into the cabin to bring up some food. Cold ham. Hard-boiled eggs again. Rolls. And a big tin of sliced peaches. What a lovely meal when you were terribly hungry!

"Chocolate to follow if anyone's hungry still," said Jill. "Mother seems to have put in dozens of bars! There's some with fruit and nuts in too. It looks gorgeous."

"Have we time to eat our dinner before we go, or had we better set sail straight away?" asked Tom, who felt that he would like to have his meal then and there. Andy looked at the sun in the sky.

"The sun's a good way past noon," he said. "I think we'd better set off now, and eat our dinner as we go. The wind won't help us so much going back, though it's shifted a bit. I'll take the tiller again."

The two boys rowed the boat out of the pool and into

the open sea. Soon they were speeding along again, though not so fast as they had come. It was very pleasant on deck in the warm afternoon sunshine. The four children ploughed their way hungrily through the ham, bread, eggs and peaches. Only Tom could manage the chocolate at the end, and even he ate it lazily, as though he didn't really want it!

"We'll be back just before dark, I think," said Andy. "Look, here's the channel between the rocks—and that's where it goes off to Smuggler's Rock. See?"

The children looked at the water that lay smoothly in the channel between the two ridges of rock, and screwed up their eyes to have another look at the queer, steep rocky island called Smuggler's Rock. Yes, there it was in the distance, a desolate, lonely rock, where nobody ever went to nowadays. It might be rather fun to explore it though!

"Shall we go there one day, Andy?" asked Tom. "It might be rather fun. We could hunt for the old caves the smugglers used."

"All right," said Andy. "If you like. It's a nice sailing trip all the way here. Doesn't the boat go like a bird?"

She did. She was light and sweet to handle and seemed like a live thing to the children. They loved the flapping of her sail and the creaking noise she made. They liked the lapping of the water against her hull, and the white wake that spread behind them like a feathery tail.

"I think all children ought to have a boat of their own," said Tom. "I wish I had a boat, and a horse and a dog, and . . ."

He stopped suddenly, and looked so upset that the two girls felt alarmed.

"What's the matter?" said Jill.

"Do you know what I've done?" said Tom. "I've left my camera behind! I'm always doing that! My best camera, the one Daddy gave me at Christmas. It cost an awful lot of money and I promised faithfully to be much more careful with it than I was with my old one. And now I've gone and left it behind, on the Cliff of Birds! "

"Idiot! " said Mary. "You're jolly careless. Mother will be awfully cross."

"Well, one of you might have been clever enough to notice I'd left it behind," said Tom crossly. "Haven't got eyes, I suppose! Dash! Andy, can we turn back?"

"What! Turn back, and climb all the way up that cliff again!" said Andy. "Don't be stupid. We haven't got time, you know that. I'm not steering this boat home in the dark through these dangerous waters."

"I didn't take any snaps, and now I've left my camera," lamented Tom. "It's such a beauty too. I must have left it at the back of that shallow cave where we lay and rested. Golly—I hope that whistling man doesn't find it and take it!"

This was a really alarming thought. Everybody looked solemn at once. A camera as fine as Tom's was very valuable, and a treasured possession. Tom couldn't think how he had come to forget it. But Tom did do very foolish things at times. How cross his parents would be!

Tom looked so woebegone that Andy was sorry for him. "Cheer up," he said. "We'll go back for it one day this week. If I can get my father to spare the boat, we'll sail to the Cliff of Birds again—and maybe visit Smuggler's Rock!"

Everyone cheered up. That would be lovely! They would start off even earlier—or would Mother let them spend the night on board the boat? Then they could have a whole day on Smuggler's Rock! They began to talk about it, their eyes shining.

"Don't be too hopeful," said Andy, steering the boat deftly between the two dangerous ridges of rock. "You know what happened last time your mother gave you permission to spend a night or two on a sailing trip—we got wrecked and lived on an island for ages, and found ourselves in a nest of enemy submarines and seaplanes!"

"Well, nothing like that could happen *here*," said Tom, looking at the desolate, lonely coast they were passing. "Why, there isn't a ship or a 'plane to be seen."

"Then I wonder what that man was looking for, with his glasses," said Jill. That made everyone remember the whistling man.

They began to talk again about the puzzle of how he could have disappeared between the place where the children sat and the waterfall.

"I tell you, there wasn't a hole big enough on the way to hide even a rabbit," said Tom. "He ought to have been somewhere along there—and he wasn't. He had vanished into thin air! I almost thought I'd dreamt him!"

"Well, he came back again from thin air all right!" said Mary, with a laugh. "We heard his whistle just as we were leaving. His hiding-place can't be far away."

The puzzle of the man's hiding-place kept them interested for a long time. It was Jill who made the first sensible suggestion.

"I know!" she said, sitting upright on the deck. "I know where he went!"

"You don't!" said Tom.

"I bet he waited till the waterfall lessened its torrent a bit—like you said it did, you remember—and then he shot into the opening the water pours from, and made his way into the cliff from there!" said Jill triumphantly. But the others hardly took in what she said, it seemed so queer.

"What—do you mean you think the man got into the cliff through the waterfall opening!" said Tom at last. "What an idea! He'd never hide there. He'd be wet through."

"Well—where did he hide, then?" said Jill. "You can't think of anywhere better, I'm sure. I dare say there's a way into the heart of the cliff just there. I'm sure there is!"

Jill was very pleased with her idea. She went on talking about it, and gradually she got the others excited. "Jill may be right," said Andy, his eyes fixed on the blue waters ahead of him. "It's true that it might be possible to get in at the waterfall hole, once the water had lessened and become a trickle—as it did when we were walking away from it."

"Let's go and see when we go back for Tom's camera!" said Mary. "We must! I simply can't bear an unsolved mystery. I can't bear not to know where that whistling man went to—and what he is doing there, too!"

"What horrid legs he had!" said Jill. "I'd like to find out his hiding-place and who he is—but I don't want to have anything to do with him at all!"

"We'll keep out of his way all right," said Andy. "Here, Tom would you like to take the tiller for a little while? It's easy going for a bit."

Tom took the tiller eagerly. The girls, suddenly feeling sleepy, lay down on rugs on the deck. It was lovely to feel the hot noonday sun. The boat careered on joyously. She always seemed to enjoy her trips so much.

"She's a happy boat," said Jill drowsily. "She likes us

coming out in her. This is a day off for her. Golly, I do feel sleepy. Wake me up at tea-time, somebody!"

They had tea at five o'clock, when the sun was sliding down the western sky. The wind whipped the sea into little waves and the *Andy* dipped up and down joyfully. The children were all very good sailors, and it didn't even occur to them to feel seasick. The sun went behind clouds and an evening chill crept over the sea. Everyone put on on extra coat and then a mackintosh. After all, it was only April!

"We'll be home before it's dark," said Tom, looking at the sinking sun. "We've had a lovely day on the sea. It was fun climbing up that cliff too, and seeing all those birds."

"And it will be fun to go back and see if there really is a hiding-place behind that waterfall," said Jill. "And I shall *love* going to Smuggler's Rock. When can we go, Andy?"

"I think the weather's changing a bit," said Andy, looking at the sky. "There'll be rain and squalls to-morrow and maybe for the rest of the week. We must choose a fine day to go off again. It would be a most uncomfortable trip in bad weather."

They got in before dark, with big clouds sweeping overhead and heavy drops of rain falling. Their mother was most relieved to see them. But she was very upset when she heard that Tom had left his camera behind.

"You will have to go and get it," she said. "It's much too good a one to leave lying about. How careless you are, Tom! It's not a bit of good giving you anything nice!"

"I'm most awfully sorry, Mother," said Tom. "I promise you we'll go and get it the very first fine day we have. Andy says the weather's broken for a while—but as soon as it's fine again, we'll go off and get my camera."

"And find that hiding-place and see Smuggler's Rock," said Jill under her breath. "Mary, don't you hope Mother lets us stay away for a night? Then we can explore Smuggler's Rock properly!"

Sailing Away Again

THE next few days, as Andy had foretold, were wet and squally. But fishing was good, and the children, in macks, rubber boots and sou'-westers, had a lovely time helping with the fish. Andy worked hard. The hauls were excellent and his father was pleased.

"Maybe he'll give me two or three days off," said Andy. "When the fine weather comes back we'll take the *Andy* and go off again. I like that better than anything."

Andy's father came to supper one night. The children's mother liked the silent, stern-faced man, and gave him a very fine supper. The children shared in it, and chattered like magpies.

"They must make your head ache!" their mother said to Andy's silent father.

"Och, their chatter is no more than the calling of the gulls!" said the fisherman, with a twinkle.

"But we're much more useful than the gulls!" said Mary. "We've helped you a lot this week. You said we had!"

"So you have," said the fisherman. "Andy's taught you a bonny lot of things! You're right good children. You don't mess about and get into mischief like most silly little scallywags."

This was a long and handsome speech from Andy's father. The children were delighted. Jill made the most of his good temper.

"Will you be able to let Andy off for a day or two soon?" she asked. "We do so want to go out in the *Andy* again all by ourselves."

"I'll give him a two-days' holiday," said the fisherman, drawing out his pipe. "May I smoke, ma'am? Thank you."

"Thanks, Dad," said Andy.

"We'll go to Smuggler's Rock then!" said Tom. "Hurrah!"

"Where's that?" asked his mother quickly.

"Oh, it's a place we saw the other day when we went to the Cliff of Birds," said Tom airily. "Mother, as Andy will have two days off, could we spend the whole time on the boat? I'd like to go to the Cliff of Birds and have time to take some proper snaps—if only I can find my camera again—and we do want to sail to Smuggler's Rock. It looks exciting."

"Not a *night* away!" began his mother. "You know I don't like that."

"But Andy will be with us. He'll look after us, won't he?" said Tom, turning to Andy's father, who was now puffing out big clouds of thick smoke. "Andy's often out all night with you, isn't he?"

"Oh, Andy's used to being on the boat for nights on end!" said the fisherman, in a very good temper after his fine supper. "You'll not come to any harm with Andy there. You can trust my boy, ma'am."

"Oh, I know I can," said the children's mother. "It's only that—well—after their adventure last year I just don't feel I want them to go travelling on their own again."

"Why, ma'am—you don't suppose two adventures like that could happen, do you?" said Andy's father. "Theirs was an adventure that only happens once in a lifetime, if that! You let them go—they'll be all right with Andy. He can anchor the boat somewhere quiet, and they can sleep on her in comfort if they take plenty of rugs."

It all seemed to be settled without any argument or difficulty at all. How lovely! The children glowed with pleasure and felt very grateful to Andy's father for making things easy for them. He seemed to have conquered their mother's fears completely!

The next evening Andy came up to the cottage. "Weather's changing," he said. "See that sky? We'll set off to-morrow, shall we? Get what food you can and I'll bring some too. Knowing young Tom's appetite I reckon we'd better lay in a good stock for two days and a night!"

Their mother always kept a fine stock of tinned food handy, and she told the children to take what they wanted. They took her at her word and soon the *Andy* was well stocked with all kinds of things, from sardines to tins of pineapple. Andy brought a few offerings too, and stared in surprise at the store already in the cabin cupboards.

"We shan't want all that!" he said. "Well—never mind —we won't bother to take it back again now. Got some rugs? We'll want plenty to sleep on. The girls can sleep down in the cabin to-morrow night—and we boys will sleep up on deck. I can rig up a tarpaulin round us to keep the wind off."

Soon there were piles of rugs on board the *Andy* too, and some of the old cushions from the cottage. It was almost dark before the children had finished stocking the little boat. They felt as if they were going on a long, long trip—a night away from home made all the difference!

They set off at eight o'clock in the morning, and their mother came down to the jetty to wave good-bye. "Have a lovely trip, and take some fine pictures, and find plenty of smugglers on Smuggler's Rock!" she said. "Tom and Andy, be sure you look after the twins well."

"Of course!" said the boys. Andy took the tiller, and the little boat glided away with the morning sun on her. Tiny white-topped waves curled against her smooth sides, and she bobbed a little.

"She's happy again!" said Jill. "And so are we! Good-bye, Mother! See you to-morrow evening!"

Soon the boat rounded the corner of the rocky bay, and was out of sight. The children settled down comfortably to enjoy the trip. They all loved the sea, and were at home on it. They watched the sea-gulls soaring in the wind. They saw them floating on the water, bobbing over the curling waves. Now for a lovely trip!

The wind was strong and the *Andy* galloped along. Mary, who had lain awake from excitement the night before, fell asleep. Spray splashed over her, but she did not wake. The others talked, and Jill once more aired her views about the hiding-place which she felt sure must be behind the waterfall.

"What I really want to know," said Tom, "is where I left my camera. I'm pretty certain I put it down in that shallow cave where we rested. I hope to goodness it's there."

Now they were running along the channel between the ridges of rocks. Later they would sight Smuggler's Rock in the distance. But they would not go there to-day. They would go to-morrow!

They turned into the shallow bay they had anchored in before, and at once there came to their ears the terrific clamour of the thousands of nesting sea-birds. "I shan't look at the cliff and see their eggs falling this time," said Jill. "Careless birds! I wonder how they know their own eggs—and what do they think when they fly back and see that they are gone?"

"Just lay some more, I suppose," said Tom. "Mary, wake up! We're there! You've been asleep for ages."

"We'll anchor in that deep pool again," said Andy, and very soon the anchor was going down with a splash.

There was no one about. The place seemed as deserted as before, except for the noisy sea-birds. But perhaps the whistling man was in hiding somewhere? Or maybe he had gone.

"Let's take some food with us and go up to that place we rested in before," said Andy. "We could have a picnic there. It's a marvellous view, right over the sea. Maybe we shall find your camera, Tom, and you can take some photographs."

Everyone thought this was a good idea, and they collected what food they wanted, and put it into kit-bags which the two boys slung over their shoulders.

"Now, don't look down at all this time, Jill," said Andy. "That's always a mistake when you're climbing. Look upwards all the time. Ready, everyone?"

Yes, they were ready. They began their steep climb up, following the cat-like Andy, who seemed to know all the best handholds and footholds. Jill didn't look down once and was quite all right. Soon they were all panting and puffing, for the day was warm.

They were glad when they reached the place where they had rested before. Jill threw herself down, tired. Tom gave a delighted exclamation and picked up his camera, which lay at the back of the shallow cave, where he had put it a few days before.

"Look! It's here! What a bit of luck. I should think that whistling man's gone, or he'd have seen it and taken it. Golly, I *am* pleased I've got it again."

They had a large and leisurely meal on the wide ledge,

35

marvelling at the great expanse of slowly moving blue sea below them. Gulls moved like white specks, and their mewing voices came on the wind all the time.

"You could easily take some photographs of the birds on their eggs," said Jill. "They come back to them very quickly."

"I'm glad we haven't got those horrid hairy legs to look at this time!" said Mary, lying down flat. "Golly, I'm sleepy again!"

"Well, don't go to sleep, because we want to go and have a look at that waterfall rushing out of the cliff," said Jill, giving her some little digs.

"Yes, come on," said Andy, getting up. "And be careful along this next path, because it's jolly narrow in places. You come just behind me, Jill, in case you get giddy."

They all went along the ledge that led round the rocky cliff to the left of their resting-place. They looked out for the waterfall. It was there all right—but the torrent was not nearly so powerful as before. It was a mere trickle compared with what it had been the other day.

"Funny!" said Andy. "I should have thought that with all the rain we've had the waterfall would be pretty big. Come along. We don't need to be afraid of being thrown off the cliff by *that* bit of water! It's no more than a gushing spring at the moment!"

They made their way to the waterfall. Beyond it the cliff-ledge along which they were walking came to a sudden end. There was no way the other side at all. The water ran out of a hole in the cliff, and fell headlong down. Andy made his way cautiously there and looked into the opening.

He gave a shout. "Anyone could get in here now! Anyone! I bet that's where the man went. He waited till the torrent lessened, then hopped up. That was his hiding-place."

"But what's he hiding for?" said Jill, puzzled. "There's nothing and no one to hide from here!"

"Can we get in?" asked Tom excitedly. "Yes, I bet we can."

"No, you're not to," said Andy. "Suppose the water came out again in a sudden great rush? You'd be sent right off the cliff, you idiot! I can't allow anything like that."

Tom looked sulky. "All right," he said, and turned back. "Well, that puzzle's solved. That's where the man went. But if you're not going to let us explore any farther, we shan't know what kind of a hidey-hole he's got or anything about him. You're a spoil-sport!"

"Can't help it," said Andy, giving him a cross little shove. "I'm in charge. Go and take some pictures of the birds while the sun is so bright!"

Tom said nothing more. But he made up his mind that as soon as the others were not looking, he would go back to the waterfall and find out a bit more for himself. He'd climb right in if he wanted to! He'd show Andy he would have his own way!

Tom is Disobedient

"I'D like to climb down the cliff again and explore the rocks at the bottom," said Jill, as they all turned back from the waterfall. "I'd like to go to where that underground river comes rushing out of the cliff too. It looks exciting down there."

"Yes, let's do that," said Mary. "It will be nice to get out of the wind a bit too. It's rather cold up here to-day."

"Right. Let's go down again then," said Andy. "Coming, Tom?"

But Tom had other ideas. He called back. "No—I don't think I'll come. I'll try and get some pictures of the birds now I'm up here and have found my camera again. I'll join you later. I'd rather try to take snapshots alone—the birds may not settle quietly with us all about."

"Well—don't be too long!" called back Jill, beginning to go down the cliff-edge with Andy just in front of her. "And for goodness' sake don't forget your camera *this* time, Tom!"

Tom sat down and looked at the gulls and other seabirds soaring and gliding in the current of air that blew straight up the cliff. They were magnificent, and Tom wished he too could spread great white wings and go gliding and circling on the strong breeze. It must be a wonderful feeling, he thought.

He could hear the voices of the others coming up to him on the wind, as they climbed slowly down. Then the gulls began suddenly clamouring all together, as they had a habit of doing, and he could hear nothing else.

"I'd better take a few pictures first, before I try any exploring up that waterfall hole," thought Tom. So he crept round the ledge, and waited till the sea-birds he had disturbed had come back again to their eggs there, and were sitting on them.

He took a few pictures that he thought should be very good. Then he put his camera down at the back of the shallow cave where they had had their meal, and made his way round the cliff to where the waterfall was.

His heart beat fast. He knew that Andy would be cross if he found out that he was going to disobey orders. "But after all, I'm thirteen, and quite able to look after myself!" thought Tom. "I'm surprised Andy hadn't the spunk to go into that waterfall hole himself! Golly, won't the others stare when they find I've been into the hole and found out where that whistling man hid the other day!"

He came to the waterfall. It was still not much more than a gushing spring now. There didn't seem any danger of a great torrent of water pouring out, as there had been the other day.

Tom peered cautiously into the opening out of which the water poured. It flowed out of a rocky bed, and had made quite a channel for itself there. Beyond, as far as Tom could see, was a ledge above the water. Anyone getting up there should be safe and dry.

He felt in his pocket. Yes, he had his torch there. It was wrapped in a few layers of thin oilskin, so that spray or splashes of sea-water would not wet it. He would need it once he got into that waterfall hole!

He climbed into the rocky hole. It was high but narrow. The water wetted him as he went in, but he didn't mind that. He dragged himself through the water and up on to the rocky ledge that lay above it.

Now he was safe from the water—unless, of course, the torrent suddenly grew bigger for some reason, and swept out of the hole, filling the opening completely, as it had done when the children had first seen it. Tom shivered a little as he thought of that. It wouldn't be pleasant for him if that happened! He had better get a bit farther inside, then he would feel safer!

He switched on his torch, and looked up the dark tunnel down which the water came. It flowed in the rocky channel it had hollowed out for itself during the long years, and beside it was the narrow rocky ledge, a continuation of the one that Tom lay on at the moment.

"I'll just explore a little way," thought the boy, feeling excited. "Just to see if I can find that man's hiding-place! I might find something there that would tell me what he is —it seems so funny for a man to be living in this desolate place. Perhaps he is hiding from the police!"

He began to wriggle along the narrow ledge. The roof of the queer little tunnel was low, and it wasn't very comfortable to wriggle along like that. Tom put his torch in his teeth so that he might have both hands to grasp the rock with and pull himself along.

The ledge ran for a few yards, and then dipped a little, so that the water ran over it! Bother! Couldn't he get any farther? Tom took his torch out of his mouth and flashed it beyond him. He saw that not far in front the narrow rocky tunnel seemed to open out—into a cave perhaps? He really *must* go and see, even if it meant a wetting!

This time he had to wriggle through the water on the ledge, and he got the front of himself very wet indeed. But he was very excited now, and didn't even feel the icy cold. He wriggled along, and found that, quite suddenly, the narrow tunnel stopped, and beyond was a very large cave, in the very heart of the cliff itself! How extraordinary!

Along the floor of the cave, almost level with the rocky floor, flowed the stream that entered the rocky tunnel, and became the waterfall! It was a strange sight to see the silent water flowing in the darkness, coming from goodness knew where.

Tom flashed his torch round the cave. This would make a fine hiding-place! This must surely be where that man had gone to. But there didn't seem to be a sign of anyone at all.

It was silent there in the heart of the towering cliff. No sound of calling sea-birds came in through the long narrow entrance. No rush of wind disturbed the still air. It was like being in a curious dream.

"I wish the others were here," thought Tom. "I'd like them to share this with me. I'll go and get them! But first I'll just flash my torch all round the cave to see if I can find even a small trace of that whistling man—a cigarette end perhaps—or a match."

He flashed his torch about. The cave had a high rocky roof, an uneven rocky floor, and gleaming walls. The water that flowed silently through it came from what looked like the entrance to a smaller cave at the back—but somehow Tom didn't want to go any deeper into the black darkness!

Something gleamed on the floor near the water. Tom's

torch shone on it, and he wondered what it was. He went to pick it up.

It was a small pearl button, the kind that is sewn on to men's shirts! But it was red, not white. Tom looked at it eagerly. Ah—that was a sure sign that somebody used the waterfall hole and had come into this cave. But it was plain that they didn't live here, for there was no sign of any food-stores, or bed. Whoever came here or made it his hiding-place must have gone farther into the cliff. Perhaps the whole cliff was honeycombed with caves and tunnels! Tom remembered the underground river that flowed out so turbulently at the foot. That must come down winding channels of its own from somewhere!

He wished very much that Andy was with him. He couldn't make up his mind whether to go farther in or not. He was afraid of being caught by the whistling man —or anyone else! The whistling man might not be the only person in the cliff. There might be someone else too.

"I don't know—I think I'll go back to the others after all," said Tom to himself. "It's a bit frightening being here in this cliff all by myself—and if I go farther in I might get lost. I'll go back."

He flashed his torch round the cave once more—and then suddenly noticed that the stream flowing in its channel across the floor of the cave, had quietly risen higher! It was now flowing over the rocky floor, almost reaching to where Tom stood.

"Look at that!" said Tom in surprise, and he stood watching the water. "Why has it risen like that? Golly, it's flooding all the floor of this cave!"

So it was. The water rose higher and swept over the floor. It began to make a noise. Tom felt alarmed.

"Gracious! I know what's happening! The torrent of water farther in must have suddenly been increased for some reason—and it's pushing its way out here—and will make that waterfall simply enormous again! If I don't go now I'll be swept out with the torrent and go down the cliff in the waterfall!"

This was not at all a pleasant thought. Tom ran over the flooding cave-floor back to the narrow tunnel into which the water flowed on its way to the open air. But already the narrow little tunnel was filling with water! The rocky ledge he had wriggled along could hardly be seen, for the water had risen high above it. In a few minutes the whole of the narrow opening would be blocked by the suddenly increased torrent of water!

"I daren't go along it now," thought Tom. "I simply daren't. I'd either be drowned or swept out and down the waterfall."

The water had now flooded the whole of the floor of the cave. It was up to Tom's knees. He felt frightened. Had he better go to the inner cave, the one his torch had shown him when he had flashed it on the water at the farther side of his cave? Perhaps he had. It wasn't safe in his cave now! Goodness knew how high the water would rise there, and there was no place he could climb up to and sit until the water went down again.

"I wish I hadn't explored in here," he thought in dismay. "Now I may be kept a prisoner for hours. The others will get worried about me. What an idiot I am!"

He made his way to the farther side of the cave he was in. Through a fairly high tunnel there the water came from an inner cave. Tom stepped into the water. It was up to his waist already. He would have to wade along until he came to the inner cave.

It was not very far in—only a matter of a few yards. Water flooded over the floor of this cave too—but to Tom's surprise and delight, he saw rough steps cut in the wall, going upwards, at the back of this inner cave. He flashed his torch there. Yes, those steps led to an opening in the cave-roof. If he got up there he would be quite safe from the rising water. Good!

"Wonder if the steps lead into another cave!" thought the boy. "This is all very weird. Who would have guessed there were these caves leading one out of the other like this, in the heart of that enormous cliff!"

He went up the rough rocky steps. There was a hole in the roof, and iron footholds had been driven into the rock there, to act as a help in the climb. Tom put his torch between his teeth again, and hauled himself up. He came out into a dark and silent tunnel, that twisted in front of him, leading to he knew not where!

"Well—I suppose I'd better go along." thought Tom, trying to sound much braver than he felt. "It must lead *some*where!"

The Hidden Cave

TOM went down the winding passage. It smelt funny, and he didn't like it. He hoped his torch wouldn't suddenly go out. He was glad that it had a new battery in! It would be horrid to wander about in the dark, inside the cliff all by himself!

The tunnel twisted downwards. It was narrow most of the time, and sometimes the roof went low so that Tom had to bend his head or he would have bumped it. Sometimes the roof became so high that Tom's torch showed him nothing but darkness. It was all very queer.

"I'd be enjoying this more if only the others were here!" thought Tom, still trying to feel brave. "I do so hope this tunnel *leads* somewhere! I almost wish I could meet that whistling man. I'd at least have someone to talk to!"

But he met nobody. The tunnel went on and on, always downwards. And then, stealing up it, came a curious, familiar smell!

Tom sniffed. "Tobacco smoke!" he thought. "Gracious! Somebody must be near then—somebody smoking a cigarette or pipe. I'd better go carefully."

He trod as quietly as he could, shading the light of his torch with his hand. Then suddenly he switched it out. He could see a light in the distance! The tunnel must come out into a cave again, he thought—and there was a light in that cave, which meant that people must be there!

He crept nearer. He could hear voices now—men's voices. One of them was the growly voice of the man with the hairy legs. Tom didn't know what he was like to look at of course, because he had only seen his legs. But he knew that growly voice again, although he had only heard the man say a few words up on the cliff.

The boy's heart began to thump. He was very glad indeed to think that people were near—but somehow he

Tom peeped cautiously into the cave

felt that they wouldn't welcome him at all! Could they be smugglers?

He tiptoed to the end of the tunnel, and peeped cautiously into the cave. Two men were there—one of them plainly the hairy-legged man, for his legs were bare, and Tom could see his enormous feet. The boy gazed at the men, wondering if they would be angry at his sudden appearance or not.

He somehow thought they would not welcome him at all. The hairy-legged man was not the giant the children had imagined him to be—he was a curious-looking fellow, with a strong, stumpy body, hairy bare arms, a big head with hardly any neck, and a flaming red beard.

The other man looked like an ordinary fisherman, but wore something that fishermen rarely wore—a pair of spectacles! They looked odd on his extremely brown face.

The men sat on boxes, talking. Tom could not hear what they were saying. He stared round the cave, astonished, for the sides of it were piled with wooden boxes and crates. Tom couldn't imagine what was in them. This was clearly a store-house of some kind. But why? And where did all the boxes come from?

There was a rough mattress in one corner of the cave. One or both men slept there, then. What a curious place to live in! Tom was completely puzzled by it all. But he did feel certain of one thing—that these men would not welcome his presence there at all! Whatever they were doing was something secret and private, something they wanted to be kept hidden.

"I daren't go in and ask them for help," thought the boy desperately. "I simply daren't. I hate the look of that man with the hairy legs. He looks as if he'd think as little of hurling me down the cliff, as of dropping and smashing those birds' eggs!"

He strained his ears to hear what they were saying. But he couldn't make out a word. Perhaps they were talking in some foreign language. Certainly the man in the fisherman's clothes, the one wearing glasses, looked like a foreigner. It was all most extraordinary.

Tom wondered if he could possibly be in some sort of very real dream. Then he got another whiff of tobacco smoke and knew he wasn't. Things never smelt as strong as that in dreams!

One of the men looked at his watch. He got up and jerked his head at the other. They made their way to a hole in the ground that Tom could not see clearly from where he stood, and seemed to drop right down. At any rate, they completely disappeared!

Tom waited a few moments and then cautiously crossed the floor of the cave and looked down the hole. There was nothing to be seen. The men had gone. Tom didn't feel at all inclined to follow them. For one thing he couldn't see how to get down the hole! There were no steps or footholds of any sort that he could see!

He looked round the cave. He could hardly see its walls, they were stacked so high with boxes of all sizes. What could be inside them?

The men had left a lantern burning on a box in the middle of the cave. Did that mean they were soon coming back? Perhaps it did. Tom felt that it would be a good thing if he were not there when they returned.

But where could he go? He stood still in the cave, thinking—and as he stood there, he heard a muffled sound. It seemed to come from somewhere to the left of the big cave.

"It's a kind of rushing watery sound," thought Tom. "Whatever can it be?"

There was a big stack of boxes on the left of the cave. Tom went to them, and saw the wall of the cave behind them. There was a hole in the wall, almost round, just about as high as Tom's waist. The rushing noise came from there.

Tom poked his head through the hole. He switched his torch on—and saw a strange sight. An underground river flowed there, swift and rushing!

"Why—that must be the river that comes out at the foot of the cliff," thought Tom. "Golly—if I could follow it, I'd soon be out of here!"

He stood and gazed at the swiftly-flowing river by the light of his torch. The dark, strong torrent moved quickly. Tom wondered how far from the foot of the cliff it was. After all, the winding, twisting tunnel he had followed had come down and down and down—maybe he was almost level with the base of the cliff now, and this river would take him very quickly to the shallow bay outside, and the sunshine.

He went back into the lamp-lit cave and looked round. He hoped that he might see another torch that he could take with him. He felt sure his own would not last much longer! He didn't want to face another long journey without being sure he had plenty of light for it!

Before he could see anything in the shape of a torch, something startling happened. There came the sound of someone scrambling up the hole in the cave floor, down which the men had gone—and, before Tom's alarmed eyes, the big, bearded face of the man with the hairy legs popped up out of the hole!

Tom stared at him, petrified—and he stared back at Tom as if he really couldn't believe his eyes. A boy! A boy in his cave! Could he be dreaming?

Tom swallowed hard, and tried to say something, but he couldn't think what to say. The bearded face just above the hole opened its eyes wide, and then the mouth opened too, and a bellow came out.

"What you doing here?"

Tom couldn't move. His feet seemed to be growing into the ground. He watched the stumpy, short-necked man heave himself out of the hole and come towards him. He was frightened, and backed away, suddenly finding himself able to move.

He backed straight into the box on which the lamp was set. The box went over and the lamp with it. It smashed at once, flared up, and then went out. The cave was instantly in black darkness.

The bearded man began to mutter something and to feel about as if he were looking for another lamp or a candle. Tom knew that this was his only chance of escape. He ran softly behind the pile of boxes to the hole in the wall that looked out on to the underground river.

He was through the hole in a trice. He had hoped there would be a ledge there, or a rock of some kind he could hold to, whilst he flashed his torch round to see what kind of a way of escape he had chosen. But there was no rock and no ledge—only the cold, rushing river!

Tom landed in the water with a splash. He caught his breath with the coldness of it. Then he began to strike out with all his might, fearing that the bearded man might come after him.

The current of the swiftly-flowing river bore him away

rapidly. Tom let himself be taken along, keeping himself afloat quite easily, but shivering with the cold. He thought of his torch gloomily. It was in his pocket, but not wrapped up in the oilskin. It would be of no use at all now. If this underground river landed him somewhere inside the cliff again, he would be in complete darkness.

"Lost for ever!" said Tom dolefully. "Oh why did I disobey Andy? I'll never get out of this mess, never! Golly, how cold the water is!"

The river bore him along, gurgling in a deep voice as it went. It apparently ran in a deep channel of rock. Tom could not see if they were passing through caves or not, nor could he see if there were any banks of rock or sand to the river. He just had to go on with it, trying to keep his balance and not be rolled over and over like a log of wood. Once his foot struck against a jutting rock, and it was badly bruised. But there was no one to hear his cry. He bit his lip with the pain, and after that was very much afraid of being bumped against a rock again.

He grew very tired and cold. And then, just as he felt he really could not go on one moment longer, he saw a bright light in front of him, a big wide, dazzling patch of light that filled him with joy.

"Sunshine!" said Tom. "That's sunshine! I must be getting near the place where the river rushes out of the cliff. I've escaped!"

Yes—it *was* sunshine! Hurrah! Tom suddenly felt so weak with relief that he couldn't seem to keep his balance any more, and the current took him and rolled him over and over. He gasped and spluttered, striking out as best he could to hold his face and shoulders out of the swift-running water.

He was taken to where sea and river met. A big wave ran up and caught him as the river took him there. Luckily for him he was thrown sideways on to a rock, and managed to pull himself up out of reach of the water.

He couldn't move. He lay there on his back, gasping for breath, shivering and trembling, whilst just below him river and sea fought their eternal battle, as one met the other, sending up spray and foam that fell pattering down on poor tired-out Tom.

Wherever is Tom?

MEANWHILE, what were Andy, Jill and Mary doing? They had been having quite a good time, though not so exciting a time as poor Tom.

They climbed steadily down the cliff, to the great alarm of all the sea-birds whose nests they passed. Once more dozens of eggs fell into the sea, knocked in by the excited uprush of the sitting birds. Jill almost made up her mind she would never climb the cliff again! She really couldn't bear to see so many eggs wasted.

They came at last to the foot of the cliff. There were some glorious rock-pools there, full of the finest sea anemones that the children had ever seen.

"Look—here's a red anemone whose feelers are as big as a peony's petals!" said Jill. "I should think he feeds on prawns and crabs—nothing so small as a shrimp would do for *him*!"

The three explored the pools thoroughly, and disturbed some enormous crabs. "Look out!" said Andy, "a nip from a big fellow like that won't be very pleasant!"

It was warm down there at the foot of the cliff. The wind was not strong there as it was up on the cliff, and the sun felt hot. Mary glanced up at the steep, towering cliff above.

"I bet Tom's beginning to feel hungry again!" she said. "I'm hungry myself—but I suppose we'd better wait till Tom comes down. He'll come as soon as he feels hungry!"

"It shouldn't take him very long to take a few snapshots," said Andy. "I'm surprised he isn't here by now. Maybe he's watching the birds. They're as good as a show sometimes!"

"Let's go and sit near that river," said Mary. "We'll take some food there, and wait for Tom. It would be rather a nice place to have a picnic. Look how the spray flies in the air where river and sea meet on the rocks."

"Yes. Let's go and get some food and eat it there," said Jill. "I really do feel very hungry. We can give Tom a call when we see him come down the cliff."

They went to where they had anchored the boat in the deep pool. In the cabin were the plentiful stores of food they had brought with them. They rummaged about, finding it hard to choose what to take.

"Sardines, bread and butter, potted meat, hard-boiled eggs—and tinned plums," said Jill.

"No—tinned pears," said Mary. "Those are nicest of all. Here's a big tin. And where's the ginger-beer? Mother gave us plenty this time. Oh, here it is."

They took everything to a high rock overlooking the spot where river and sea met. Spray was sometimes flung as high as their rock, but they didn't mind that—it was all part of the fun to dodge it when it came!

They set out the meal, and then looked up at the side of the cliff to see if there was any sign of Tom coming down. But there wasn't.

"What *can* he be doing?" said Jill impatiently. "He's been ages!"

"Well—we'll wait five minutes more, and then begin without him," said Mary. "And if there's nothing left he'll jolly well have to go and get something else himself!"

They waited for five minutes, but still there was no Tom. Andy looked a little worried, but he said nothing. They opened the sardines, spread butter on their bread, and began a delicious meal. By the end of it there was not much left—and still no Tom!

"Andy—you don't think Tom's in any difficulty up there, do you?" said Jill suddenly. "It's so unlike him not to turn up long before a meal-time."

"Well—I've been wondering about that myself," said Andy. "I think I'd better go up the cliff again and fetch him down. He may have gone to sleep."

"What a nuisance he is!" said Mary. "Poor Andy— having all that climb again!"

"Oh, I don't mind," said Andy. "Now you girls stay here till we come. It's nice and sunny, and you're not much bothered with the wind. I'll be as quick as I can."

Off he went. Soon the girls could see him, small and far off, up the cliff-side, climbing steadily, the sea-birds flying wildly round his head.

"I bet he gives Tom a scolding!" said Jill, lying down on her back, enjoying the feel of the sun-warmed rock behind her. "Won't Tom be famished when he comes back!"

Andy climbed steadily, and at last came to the resting-place where they had had their dinner. There was no one there, of course—but what was this at the back? Tom's camera again! So he was *not* photographing the birds after all! Well, what was he doing then—and where was he? Andy began to feel frightened.

He left the camera where it was, and went on round the cliff, on the narrow ledge that led to the waterfall. It was now no longer a trickle, but was pouring out in a great cataract!

Andy went right up to it. An awful thought came to him. Could Tom have been foolish enough to try and get into the cliff through the waterfall hole? Surely, surely not!

"I forbade him to, anyway," said Andy, but he couldn't help feeling that Tom would have disobeyed him easily if he had wanted to badly enough. Had he gone inside? And had the water suddenly grown in volume, and closed his way out again?

Andy stood looking at the waterfall, knowing there was nothing to do for Tom, if he really had gone inside. Either the boy would have to wait till the waterfall lessened in volume again—or find some other way out. And what way was there? None, so far as Andy could see!

The boy sat there for some time. Then, thinking that he must not leave the girls alone any longer, he got up to go. But he did not feel at all happy.

As he moved away from the waterfall its noise grew less. The boy turned round and saw that once again it had lessened, until now it was no more than a gushing spring. What a queer thing it was! He turned to go on again, and then stopped, his eyes almost falling out of his head!

Out from the waterfall exit came an enormous hairy leg! Then another! Andy knew perfectly well they were the same legs he and the others had seen before. For some reason or other they filled the boy with fright. He climbed

51

hurriedly round the edge of the cliff, to be out of sight of the man when he emerged from the hole.

He climbed down steadily. He passed the place where Tom's camera was, without thinking about it. He was just below this place, clinging to a rather difficult bit of the cliff, when he heard the growling voice not far above him. Then something hurtled past him, something with a long brown strap. It flew downwards, but the sea-birds and wind were making such a noise that Andy did not hear crash or thud as the thing struck the rocks below.

He clung to the cliff-side, his heart thumping, wondering if the man would come after him, or had seen him. But apparently he had not, for no one came down the cliff-path, and all was quiet except for the sounds of wind, sea and birds.

Andy, his mind in a turmoil, climbed down the rest of the cliff as fast as he could. He knew the girls could see him, and would be watching anxiously to see if Tom were following. What *had* happened to Tom? It was terribly worrying.

He reached the girls, and found them sitting upright on their rock, looking pale and frightened.

"Couldn't find Tom," said Andy. "I think the silly little idiot's got inside the waterfall hole—and goodness knows what's happened to him. You were right, Jill, when you said that hairy-legged man made that place his hidey-hole. He came out of there when I was quite near!"

"Andy—look!" said Mary in a low, scared voice, and pointed to something on a rock not very far from them. "Look! That came down a little while ago, and made us jump terribly. It crashed on that rock—and oh, Andy —it's Tom's camera!"

Mary burst into tears. The shock of the camera falling so near, and smashing into hundreds of bits, had given her a shock. And now Andy had come back without Tom.

"Andy, what *are* we to do about Tom?" asked Jill. "Surely he wouldn't have gone exploring like that all by himself?"

"Tom can be very foolish at times," said Andy. "*Why* did I leave him up there alone? I'm afraid he may have been caught by that man. There's something queer going on here. I don't want to be mixed up in it. I want to get back home. No more adventures for me! I had enough of them last year."

"But, Andy—*Andy*—we can't go home without Tom!" said Mary, beginning to cry again. "We can't leave him here all alone."

"I'd better take you safely home, and get Dad back here to find Tom, and discover what's going on," said Andy, who looked rather white. He didn't like seeing that smashed camera. What a temper the hairy-legged man must have to fling a beautiful camera down the cliff and smash it like that! Andy remembered how the man had smashed the birds' eggs too, and he didn't at all like the thought of coming into contact with him, when he had two small girls to look after!

He stood up. "Collect the things and come back to the boat," he ordered. "We must go."

"No," said Mary. "I'm not going. I'm not going to desert Tom, if you are!"

"Don't be silly," said Andy. "We're not deserting him. We're going to get Dad and come back and find Tom. Come along. Don't argue. I'm the skipper here."

Jill began to gather up the things, but Mary was still obstinate. Andy hauled her to her feet and gave her a rough shake. "Do as you're told! Can't you see I'm worried stiff? It's Tom's disobedience that has led to this— I'm not going to have any *more* trouble! You'll come along with Jill and me straight away!"

Mary, with tears streaming down her cheeks, began to help Jill to collect the things left over from their tea. Jill, almost in tears herself, gave a last glance down at the underground river, which flowed so swiftly from the foot of the cliff. Then she stood still, her eyes wide and her mouth opened to give a cry. But none came.

She reached out her arm and pointed downwards. The others looked. Rolling over and over on the river, swept from side to side like a log, came a strange dark object.

"Andy! It's Tom—poor, poor Tom!" said Jill, in a choking voice. "It's too late to save him. The river's got him."

Very white under his brown, Andy looked down at the tumbling body. He saw it swept to one side, on to the rocks, where sea and river met. It tumbled out and lay

53

there. Then he saw how the tired arms heaved up the exhausted body to a place of safety.

"He's all right!" yelled Andy, almost startling the girls out of their skins. "He's all right. Hi, Tom, Tom, you scamp, where have you been? How did you get here?"

All three rushed down the rocks to the one where Tom lay, slipping and sliding as they went. He looked up at them and grinned feebly.

"Hello!" he said. "Nice to see you all again! I'm sorry to say that we've plunged into the middle of a most exciting adventure! You wait till I've told you everything. Anybody got anything to eat? I'm most *frightfully* hungry!"

What Happened on the Way Back

ANDY, Jill and Mary were so relieved to see Tom alive and hungry that for a moment they could only stare at him in joy, and say nothing at all. Then Jill rushed to get something for him to eat. Andy called after her. "Bring a couple of rugs. Tom's wet through and shivering."

Soon Tom was sitting in a sheltered corner, munching bread and potted meat, his wet clothes drying in the wind, and a couple of warm rugs tucked round him.

Andy wouldn't let the girls ask him any questions till he had got some food inside him and had stopped shivering. They could hardly wait to know what had happened to him. How extraordinary it had been to see Tom come rolling over and over in the restless waters of the underground river!

"Now—tell us everything!" said Jill, when Tom had finished his meal. Tom glanced at Andy, and looked rather embarrassed. He didn't like to own up to his disobedience, which had nearly brought disaster on him.

Andy saw the look. "I suppose you played the fool, and got in through the waterfall opening?" he said, not unkindly, but sternly. Tom went red and nodded.

"Yes—I did," he said. "I'm sorry, Andy. I know you're the skipper here. I just felt I *had* to. But I wished and wished I hadn't been such an idiot, once I'd got through."

"I'm very glad you're safe," said Andy. "But you listen to me, young Tom—any more disobedience from you and you don't come out in my boat any more. See? I'm in charge, and if you can't be loyal to your skipper, you're no use."

"I know, Andy. I know," said Tom humbly. "I won't

55

play the fool again. I've had my lesson. You wait till you hear!"

"*Do* tell us!" begged Jill. "Don't scold him any more, Andy. Let him tell us his story."

So Tom told them how he had wriggled through the waterfall opening, found himself in the cave, which became flooded, so that he had to make his way farther in. He told them about the rough steps leading out from the inner cave, and the long, winding, downhill passages through the heart of the cliff.

When he described finding the cave down below, used apparently as some kind of store-house, and the two men sitting there, talking, the others sat listening intently, holding their breath so as not to miss a word!

"Golly!" said Andy. "This is amazing. There's something queer going on. But what can it be? You were lucky to escape, Tom. But you must have had a shock when you fell into that swirling, underground river."

"I did," said Tom. "And wasn't it a bit of luck that it took me right out here, almost to your feet? I shouldn't have liked it much if the current had thrown me into that foaming surging bit over there, dashing over the rocks. I'd have been knocked to bits!"

"It's a pity those men know somebody is here," said Andy. "I simply can't imagine what they're up to. Can they be smugglers? But what are they doing inside this cliff? There's no road overland to take smuggled goods. It's a real puzzle."

"Do you think the men will come after us?" said Jill, looking rather scared.

"Well—they only know about Tom—and maybe they think he's fallen over the cliff now," said Andy. "It's plain they thought he had gone back up the winding passage to the waterfall opening. They must have gone up there themselves, thinking they were chasing him—and all they found was his camera on the cliff-ledge. They must have thrown it down in rage. What a shame! It's smashed to bits."

Tom was feeling much better now. In fact, he was feeling quite a hero! True, he had disobeyed Andy—but things had come out all right, and he had made some queer discoveries. He began to look a little cocky. But Andy soon put a stop to that.

"I think we ought to get back home as soon as we can," he said. "Tom's sure to get a chill after this. That river water is icy-cold. It's a pity to bring our trip to such a sudden end, but I don't want Tom down with pneumonia or something!"

Tom's face fell. "Oh, Andy—don't be such an idiot! I'm perfectly all right, you know I am."

"Anyway, Andy—isn't it too late to start back?" asked Jill, looking at the sun, which was now well down in the west.

Andy looked at it too and made some calculations. "The wind's in our favour—and we can get past the worst rocks whilst it's still daylight. I think we ought to go. Also, those two men will be on the look-out for our boat, I expect, and may try to surprise us in the night."

"Blow!" said Tom. "Why did I go and upset things like this? Spoiling our lovely trip. And we haven't been to Smuggler's Rock either!"

Once Andy had made up his mind to do something, he didn't take long to set about it. "Come on," he said, getting up. "Those men are sure to start prying around soon. We'd better go now."

They all went back to the *Andy* with sad faces. What a sudden end to what had promised to be a really exciting trip! They clambered on board and put up the red sail. The evening sun shone softly down, and the sail glowed as they pulled it up, throwing a brilliant shadow on the pale blue water.

The wind was very strong now. Andy deftly steered his boat out of the bay, her sail filling with the wind. Soon she was scudding along fast.

Nobody said anything. They were all disappointed. It was horrid to leave an unsolved mystery behind too. How they would have loved to find out why those men were in the cave, what they were doing there, and who they were! Probably they never would find out, because neither Andy's father nor the children's mother might take much notice of their excited tale.

The sun seemed to go down very quickly. Just as it was about to disappear over the western edge of the world, Tom gave a yell and pointed ahead.

"What's that?" he cried. "Look, over there, by those tall rocks."

Andy's sharp eyes made out what it was at once—a motor-boat! It was lying still, not moving. Could it be waiting for them?

There was nothing to do but go on. The *Andy* swept along, her red sail glowing. When she came near the waiting boat, they heard her motor being started up, and the boat swung out into the centre of the channel down which the *Andy* was flying.

Andy saw that he could not get past in safety. The channel between the two ridges of rock was narrow there. He would go on the rocks if he tried to swing past!

They came up to the motor-boat. A tall, foreign-looking man leaned over the side.

"Who are you? What are you doing here?" he shouted.

"That's none of your business!" shouted back Andy. "Get out of our way!"

"Anchor your boat and come on board here," ordered the tall man most surprisingly. "If you don't, we'll capture you, boat and all!"

"Who are *you*?" bellowed back Andy angrily. "Clear out of our way! We're children out on a sailing trip."

"Andy! Turn back! Let's go back to the Cliff of Rocks," begged Jill, frightened. Andy looked scornful, then seemed to alter his mind. He looked anxiously at the sky, which was now dark and overcast with the coming night and with heaped-up clouds. In a short time it would be almost dark.

The man, joined by another man, began to yell at Andy again to come on board. He could not really see if Andy's crew were children or not, for there was a little distance between the boats. Then something happened.

A great wave surged up, and took hold of the motor-boat, swinging her round violently. She must have struck a rock just below the surface, as the wave receded suddenly, for there was a grinding noise and the motor-boat shivered from top to bottom.

The two shouting men were almost thrown overboard. They disappeared at once to see what the damage was.

"Now's our chance!" said Andy. "We'll turn and go back—but not to the Cliff of Rocks, which is where they will expect to find us, I've no doubt—but to Smuggler's

Rock! You remember where this channel forks off to it? We'll take that course—and we must hope it won't be too dark for me to see it!"

So, whilst the men were trying to find out what damage had been done to their boat, the *Andy* turned round and stole off, tacking a little to get the help of the breeze. Andy did not think that the motor-boat would dare to come after them in the gathering dark, so, as soon as he could, he pulled down the sail, and took the oars, with Tom.

"Look out for the place where the channel forks," he said. "It's a good long row, but never mind!"

Fortunately the current helped them, and it was not so hard as Andy had expected. They found where the channel forked off for Smuggler's Rock, and then, to their joy, saw that the moon was sliding out from behind the thinning clouds.

"That will help a lot," said Andy. "Look—you can see the faint shape of Smuggler's Rock over there!"

They slid along the channel, which was wider here, and came nearer to the tall, steep rock. They could not see it very clearly, for it was full of shadows. They took the boat into a small cove. Andy thought they had better drop anchor there and hope for the best. He didn't think anyone would come looking for them at Smuggler's Rock. Perhaps next day they could escape out to sea.

They let down the anchor. "Are we going on to the little island?" asked Jill.

"No," said Andy. "We shouldn't be able to find our way properly, with the moon slipping in and out of clouds like this. We'll sleep on the boat—as we planned to do!"

"Can we all sleep on deck?" asked Jill.

"No—you and Mary must sleep down in the cabin," said Andy. "Have a rug each—that should keep you warm enough down there. We'll have the rest of the rugs and cushions because it will be chilly up on deck."

"I feel a bit scared now," said Mary. "I didn't like those two men yelling at us."

"You needn't be afraid," said Andy. "You will be quite safe down in the cabin—and Tom and I will take it in turns to keep guard up here in case anybody *should* come. But no one will."

Puzzled, tired, and still a bit frightened the twins went

down into the cabin. They passed up rugs and cushions to the boys. Then they settled down to sleep.

Andy said he would take the first watch, and wake Tom up in three hours. Tom, tired out with all his adventures, was asleep at once. Andy sat beside him, covered in rugs, on guard. What a curious adventure this was! Andy couldn't make head or tail of it!

A Night on the Boat

IT was a lovely night, with scudding clouds going across the moon. In the quiet cove there was very little movement of the water, and the boat hardly stirred. Andy heard the tiny lapping sounds against her sides as he kept his watch.

He puzzled over everything that had happened. Tom had said that the big cave inside the cliff, at the foot, where the underground river rushed by, was stored with boxes and crates. Where had they come from?

"And how did the men get them there?" wondered Andy. "Surely they couldn't have taken them up that steep cliff, through the waterfall opening, and down the winding passages that Tom described? That's quite impossible. Could a motor-boat get up that rushing underground river? No—the current is much too strong—and by Tom's description of it I should think the roof is too low in parts."

No—it was too much of a puzzle and Andy soon gave up trying to solve it. "All I'm certain of is that there's something queer going on, something unlawful—and the sooner we get back now and tell the grown-ups, the better," thought Andy. "We can't possibly tackle this ourselves. And there are the girls to think of—I daren't let them run into any more danger than I can help."

When his three hours were up he woke Tom. It was hard to wake him, for the boy was really tired out after all his adventures that day. Still, he was soon sitting up straight, the rugs well wrapped round him, looking out on the moonlit cove.

"Three hours, Tom—then wake me again," said Andy, snuggling down in the rugs as close to Tom as he could, for warmth. It was a chilly night.

Tom felt terribly sleepy. He found that his head was nodding and his eyes were closing. That would never do! To go to sleep when guarding the others would be a real crime—he couldn't possibly do that. Andy would never, never trust him again.

"I'd better walk about a bit," said Tom to himself. He cautiously wriggled out of his rugs so as not to wake Andy, and paced the deck. He thought he heard a movement down below, and he opened the cabin-hatch softly.

"Are you all right down there?" he said in a whisper.

Mary's voice answered him. "I can't go to sleep, Tom, I've tried and tried. I simply can't. Let me come up on deck with you a bit and keep watch. I'm sure Andy wouldn't mind. I'll bring up some chocolate."

Chocolate sounded pretty good to Tom. He called back softly. "Well, don't wake Jill. Come on up and bring your rug. Just for a little while."

Mary came up into the moonlight, dragging her rug with her. She looked round.

"Oh—isn't it lovely up here with the moonlight making the sea all silvery. What black shadows there are in Smuggler's Rock! I wonder if we'll have time to explore it to-morrow. Here's your chocolate, Tom."

They sat down together, cuddling into the thick rugs. They munched the chocolate, which tasted delicious, eaten in the middle of the night like that! Tom felt quite wide awake by now. He and Mary began to discuss the day's happenings in low tones, so as not to wake Andy.

"Did you get your torch wet?" asked Mary. "You know —when you fell into the underground river?"

"Yes, I did," said Tom, and felt in his pocket for it. "I expect it's quite spoilt. I'll try it."

He pressed the little button that usually set the torch alight—but nothing happened. It was quite spoilt. Tom put it back into his pocket again. As he did so he felt something else there—a tiny round thing. What was it?

He took it out. It was the little red pearl button he had found on the floor of one of the caves. He showed it to Mary.

"Look," he said. "I forgot about this. I found it on the floor of the cave behind the waterfall. That's what made me feel certain the hairy-legged man must hide somewhere

Tom showed the little red button to Mary

in the cliff. After all, a button means a shirt or a vest, doesn't it?"

"Did he wear a red shirt when you saw him in the hidden cave far below?" asked Mary, turning the red button over in her hand.

"No. I don't think so," said Tom, trying to remember. "I don't think the other fellow did, either. He was dressed like a fisherman. I didn't much like the look of either of them."

He put the button back into his pocket, and the two fell silent, enjoying the soft motion of the little boat and the wisha-wisha noise that the water made against her. Mary thought it was such a lovely sound. She bent over the side and dabbled her hand in the water.

"Awfully cold," she said, and yawned. "Have you finished your chocolate? I think I'll go back now. I feel sleepy. I don't think anything will happen to-night, Tom. We're quite safe here."

She went below, taking her rug with her. Tom had no fear of falling asleep now. He felt wide awake. He looked at Smuggler's Rock. What a tall, steep, rocky place it was! He felt sure that there would be heaps of sea-birds nesting there too. He hoped Andy wouldn't rush them all away in the morning, without letting them land on the island and have a look at it.

The moon went behind a cloud. At once Smuggler's Rock became dark and black. Tom glanced idly at the top of it—and then he straightened himself up suddenly, and looked very sharply at something.

"There's a light of some sort up there!" he said under his breath. "Yes—there it is again—flash, flash, flash! Somebody's signalling from there. Gracious, are there people here too?"

The light went on flashing. Tom woke Andy by shaking him roughly. The fisher-boy awoke at once and sat up in alarm, expecting he knew not what.

"Look, Andy, look—there's a light flashing at the very top of Smuggler's Rock!" said Tom. "Up there, see. Can you see it? It's a signal of some sort, I should think."

Andy looked. He soon spotted the light. He watched it intently. It went on for some time and then stopped.

"What do you make of that?" said Tom.

"I don't know," said Andy. "One more puzzle added

to the other puzzles! Anyway, I'm determined to get away home as soon as possible to-morrow. We ought to report all these queer doings—and we'd better not be mixed up in them more than we can help. I don't like this kind of puzzle!"

The light did not flash any more. Andy looked at his watch, and then curled himself up. "I've got another hour of sleep," he said. "Keep a sharp look-out, Tom, and wake me if you see anything else going on."

But nothing else happened in the rest of Tom's watch, much to his disappointment. He woke Andy up at the right time, and then curled up again in the rugs himself. "I don't feel a bit sleepy," he said. "I could sit up all night now."

But he was asleep almost before Andy had walked across the deck and back. Below, in the cabin, Jill and Mary were asleep too. It was all very peaceful.

At dawn Andy woke them all. "You girls get a quick breakfast going," he ordered. "Take these rugs down, Tom. We'll start off as soon as we can."

"Which way are we going back?" asked Tom, dragging the rugs to the hatch, to drop them down to the girls.

"I'm not sure," said Andy. "If I were certain that that motor-boat had gone, I'd risk the way we know. I've no idea if we can get out to sea from here—or what is the best course to take, if we can. I wish I dared climb up to a high bit of Smuggler's Rock, and have a look-see. I can't see anything from here."

"Well, why shouldn't you climb up Smuggler's Rock, and have a look round the sea?" said Tom. "You might spot the motor-boat. You might see clearly how we could best make our way home from here."

"Have you forgotten those lights we saw flashing last night?" said Andy. "There's somebody on the island. We don't want to get caught by them. It seems as if there is a perfect network of people in this desolate part of the coast!"

"But it's so early in the morning," said Tom. "No one will be about now. Let's all have a quick breakfast, Andy, and then hop across to Smuggler's Rock quickly, climb up to that high point up there—see where I mean—and have a look-out from there. We could see for miles. I bet you'd

C

spot the motor-boat if it was lying in wait for us anywhere about here."

"Well—perhaps I'd better try and spy out the way," said Andy. "Maybe no one will be about yet, as you say. We won't talk or laugh as we go. We'll be absolutely quiet."

They sat down on the deck to have a good breakfast. This time it was hot soup out of tins, with bread, and plenty of biscuits spread with marmalade. There was hot cocoa to drink too, sweetened with condensed milk. Everybody enjoyed their queer breakfast very much indeed.

"Hot soup was a jolly good idea," said Andy to Jill, who looked pleased at his praise. "It's so jolly cold this morning. But then, it's very early—the sun is only just coming up. Look! "

They finished their breakfast watching the blue water in the cove turn to dancing gold as the sun came up. Everything looked clean and beautiful and washed, Mary said. So it did! Even the rocks gleamed in the early sun as if somebody had been along and given them a good cleaning!

Andy glanced up the steep rocks of the island nearby. "I think that high point that Tom thought would be a good one is about the best to choose," he said. "I don't quite like you girls coming, but I'd rather we were all together. We'll be as quick as we can."

They left all the breakfast things as they were, and leapt across to a nearby rock. Soon they were clambering over the shining rocks, going up as fast as they could. There were no steep cliffs as there were in the bay they had anchored in before—just masses of rocks, covered with seaweed as far as the spray reached, but dry and black beyond.

They went right up to the high point that Tom had chosen. Certainly there was a wonderful view from there. They looked all round the sea as far as they could. It was rough that morning, and white horses galloped everywhere.

There was no sign of the motor-boat to be seen. Andy looked everywhere, his hawk-like eyes ranging for miles! He had the fine sight of the fisherman, and could often see things out to sea that neither Tom nor the girls could see.

"Nothing to be seen," said Andy, pleased. "Good thing

too, because I can't for the life of me see how we would escape any other way than the one we know. I'd be afraid to sail out to sea, with all those rocks about."

"Well—let's get back home as quick as we can," said Jill, and began to leap from rock to rock downwards. Andy yelled a warning—but he was too late.

Jill slipped and fell. She tried to get up and couldn't. Andy hurried to her in great alarm. Whatever had she done?

A Horrid Shock

JILL was sitting on a rock, looking very white indeed. She nursed one of her ankles and moaned a little. Tears ran down her cheeks.

"What's up? Have you hurt your ankle?" asked Andy, kneeling down beside her. "Oh, Jill—how foolish to skip down those steep rocks like that!"

"I know. Oh, Andy, my ankle does hurt so. Oh, what shall I do?" wailed poor Jill. "I'm a baby to cry, but I can't help it."

Mary was almost crying too as she bent down by her twin. She took off Jill's rubber shoe. The ankle was already swollen.

Andy felt it tenderly. "I don't think it's a real sprain," he said. "You've just given it an awful twist. It will be all right soon. Don't walk on it just yet."

"Pull her near this pool," said Tom, seeing a big, clear pool of rain-water in the hollow of a rock. "She can put her foot into it. That will be as good as bathing it, I should think."

Jill's foot did feel better in the cold water. Soon the colour came back to her face and she rubbed away the tears. "I simply couldn't *help* crying," she said. "You can't think how awful the pain was just for the moment. But it's much better now."

The foot was still very swollen. Andy thought she had better wait a while before trying to walk on it. So they sat by the pool and talked, Andy keeping a sharp look-out in case anyone came. He told the girls about the lights he and Tom had seen the night before.

After a while Jill thought she could try to walk. Andy

helped her up, but as soon as she put her hurt foot to the ground, she gave a cry and crumpled up again. "I don't think I can—not just yet, anyway," she said.

"Well, rest a bit longer," said Andy, trying not to look worried. He did so badly want to get back home quickly. He looked down the steep stretch of rocks below, leading to the cove where the boat was. He could not see the boat, but it was quite a distance below. It wouldn't be much good trying to help Jill down the steep rocks at the moment. She would probably slip and fall again, dragging them with her. They must all wait in patience.

They looked round them. Smuggler's Rock was truly a lonely, desolate-looking place. The sea-birds did not nest there in such thousands as they did on the Cliff of Birds, but there were plenty of them about, circling in the breeze and calling loudly. The island rose to a steep pinnacle. Anyone at the very top would have a perfectly marvellous view for miles out to sea.

"I wish I could go right to the top and have a look what it's like there," said Tom longingly.

"You won't do anything of the sort!" said Andy sharply. "You got into a nice mess yesterday, and I'm not having you get into any more trouble to-day! Besides, you know perfectly well that that was where those lights showed last night. If anyone is on this island now, they would most likely be up there."

"All right, Andy, all right," said Tom. "I only just said I'd *like* to go up there. I'm not going."

It seemed a long time till Jill was able to put her foot to the ground again without too much pain. It was still swollen, but not quite so much. It wasn't a sprain, but she certainly had twisted it very badly.

"It's about half-past ten," said Andy. "If you feel you can possibly limp down now, Jill, with Tom and me helping you, we'd better go."

Jill tried her foot. Yes—if she didn't put her whole weight on to it, but held on to Tom and Andy, she thought she could manage.

They started down. It was a slow little procession that went down the rocks, taking the very easiest way so that Jill would not have to do any jumping. Twice she had to sit down and rest. Andy was gentle and patient, but inside he felt anxious and worried. Suppose anyone on the island saw them and stopped them? He was longing to get back to the boat and sail away.

They got down to the cove at last. There lay the boat, rocking gently where they had left her. But immediately they saw her the children saw that something was lacking. What was it?

"Where's the sail?" said Tom. "We left it folded on the deck at the end there. Where is it?"

Andy said nothing. His keen eyes swept the boat from end to end, and his heart went cold. Had someone taken the sail?

He left Jill to Tom and Mary, and went jumping down to the cove, landing like a sure-footed goat on the rock, beside the *Andy*. He leapt on board.

He made a hurried search, whilst the others came slowly nearer, Tom and Mary helping Jill along. He turned to them with a grim face as they came aboard.

"Do you know what's happened? Somebody's been here and taken, not only our sail, but our *oars* too!"

The three stared at him in horror. The sail gone—and the oars as well? How could they get home then?

"But, Andy—we can't go home now," said Jill, looking very pale with shock and pain.

"I'm afraid not," said Andy, and he helped Jill to a comfortable place on the deck. He looked all round searchingly, but he could see nobody at all. Who had taken the sail and the oars?

"Someone came along whilst we were up on that high point," he said. "Someone who meant to keep us here. And the easiest way to keep us was to do something that would make it impossible for us to take the boat home. So he removed the sail and the oars. If I could just get hold of him!"

Jill began to cry again. Her ankle was hurting her once more, and she was longing to get back home and be comforted by her mother. She sobbed bitterly. Andy put his arm round her.

"Poor old Jill. Never mind, we'll manage somehow—even if we have to swim home!"

But Jill couldn't smile. "You see," she sobbed, "if I hadn't been such an idiot as to jump down the rocks like that, and twist my ankle, we'd have had plenty of time to get away. It's all my fault—and my ankle hurts again—and I feel simply awful."

"You go down into the cabin and lie down," said Andy. "Mary will put a wet, cold bandage on. Tom and I will talk over things, and see what we think is best to do."

Jill managed to get down into the cabin. She was glad to lie down on the little bunk there and put her foot up. Mary wrung a bandage out in cold sea-water, and wrapped it carefully round the swollen ankle.

The boys sat up on deck and talked gravely together. Andy felt that things were serious now.

"We've stumbled on to something that those men wanted to keep secret," said Andy. "They chose this lonely, forgotten bit of coast for whatever it is they wanted to do —smuggle, I suppose. And now we've butted in and spoilt their little game."

"They'll be very angry," said Tom.

"You bet they will!" said Andy. "It's quite clear they don't mean us to get home and talk about it. They'll keep us prisoner here till they've finished their job, whatever it is. Something to do with all those crates and boxes, I suppose.

"I wonder what's in them," said Tom.

"Forbidden goods of some kind," said Andy. "It's very worrying. Your mother and my father will be very anxious when we don't turn up."

"Well, they know where we've gone," said Tom, brightening up. "They'll come and look for us. Your father will get your uncle's boat and come and see what's happened. He's sure to come to Smuggler's Rock if he doesn't find us at the Cliff of Birds."

"Yes. He will," said Andy. "But I bet our captors, whoever they are, have thought of that. They'll deal with that when the time comes."

"How?" asked Tom. "What do you mean?"

"Well, I mean that if they see Dad's boat coasting along, they'll take steps to see we're not about!" said Andy, grimly.

Tom looked scared. "What about our boat?" he said. "They can't hide that."

Andy said nothing to that. He was silent so long that Tom looked up at him. To his enormous alarm he saw what looked like one bright tear in the corner of the

71

fisherboy's eye. He was so alarmed that he caught hold of Andy's hand.

"*Andy!* Whatever's the matter? Why do you look like that?"

Andy swallowed, and blinked back the unexpected tear. "Well, idiot," he said, trying to speak naturally, "they'll probably scuttle my boat, that's all! That's the best way to hide a boat you don't want found. I think they're pretty desperate fellows, and they won't stick at sinking a boat if it suits them."

Sink the *Andy*! Scuttle their beautiful swift-running boat? Tom stared at Andy in horror. They all loved the boat, but Andy loved her most of all, because he had used her for a long time now, and knew all her little ways. All the fishermen loved their boats, of course, but this was Andy's first boat, and a beauty.

"Oh, Andy," said Tom, and couldn't think of anything else to say at all. "Oh, *Andy.*"

They said nothing for a few minutes. Then they heard Mary coming up to soak Jill's bandage again. "Don't tell the girls what we're afraid will happen," said Andy in a low voice. "No good scaring them before it happens."

"Right," said Tom. He managed to give Mary a grin as she came up. "How's Jill?"

"She says her ankle feels better now her foot is up," said Mary. "We've been talking about the oars and the sail, Tom. Couldn't we go and look for them? We might find them hidden somewhere."

"Not very likely," said Andy. "It was pretty smart work on the part of the person who came along and saw our boat. He went off with them at once."

"I do feel hungry," said Tom. "I suppose it isn't time for a meal, is it? Gracious, Andy, I've just thought of something. We've brought quite a bit of food with us, luckily—but not enough for more than two or three days. I hope we shan't starve!"

"We'll be rescued long before that," said Andy, seeing Mary's alarmed face. "Anyway, we'll have something to eat now. It's about twelve o'clock. Look at the sun!"

They had a good meal, and Andy and Tom kept a look-out all the time in case they saw anyone stealing about. But they saw no one.

"We must make up our minds to stay here for a while,"

said Andy. "And I think we'll remove all the food and rugs and things from the boat, Tom. We'll find a good little home somewhere on Smuggler's Rock—in a cave or somewhere—and make ourselves as comfortable as possible."

"Almost as if we'd been wrecked!" said Mary, feeling suddenly cheerful. "That sort of thing is fun, even if we *are* in trouble! Come on—let's find a good place."

A Good Little Home

THEY left Jill on deck, because her ankle was still painful, though very much better. She could hobble about now, and felt more cheerful. She was very disappointed not to be able to go with them and find a good sleeping-place for that night.

"But why can't we sleep on the boat?" she asked, surprised. "Like we did last night."

The boys did not like to tell her that at any moment they thought somebody might come along and scuttle the boat—sink her down to the bottom of the pool; so that it was necessary to remove everything to some good place, in order not to lose the things on the boat.

"We'd be more comfortable, I expect, if we find a sandy cove, sheltered from the wind," said Andy. "We'll keep the boat in sight, Jill, as we go, so you needn't be afraid by yourself. We'll be able to see you all the time, and you'll be able to see us."

The three of them set off. They went over the rugged rocks, keeping the *Andy* in sight all the time. The boys did not think anyone would go to the boat just then, but Andy was not going to risk leaving Jill completely alone. If they kept the boat in sight they could see what was happening at any moment.

"It's no good going the way we went this morning, up to that high point," said Andy. "For one thing the boat is out of sight from there, and for another I didn't see a single place where we could get comfort and shelter. Did you?"

"No," said Tom. "It all looked jolly hard and wind-swept and uncomfortable, I thought. Let's go the other way—look, is that green grass, over there? No, it's cushions of some kind of sea-shore plant. We might find a good spot over there, but higher up. I reckon that if a storm came the sea would sweep right over these rocks we're on now."

"Yes, it would," said Andy. "You can see bits of sea-weed here and there—clinging on in the hope of sea-water, I should think. I hope a storm *doesn't* come! That would about finish the *Andy*, lying there among those rocks. She'd be torn from her anchor, and smashed to bits."

"Well—it doesn't look as if a storm is near," said Tom, not liking this conversation at all. "It's fine to-day, though it's cold. Look, Andy—let's climb up here to that broad ledge. It looks pretty sheltered there. Is that a cave behind the ledge?"

They climbed up to the broad ledge of rock, keeping the *Andy* well in sight all the time. "We don't want to go too far from the boat," said Andy. "It would be such a fag carrying everything. If there's a cave there it would be very convenient!"

There *was* a cave—rather an awkward one with a very low roof at the front, so that the children had to crawl in almost flat. But inside it opened out into a fairly roomy cave, with a higher roof. It smelt clean and fresh, and had a sandy floor, which Andy was surprised to see.

"This will do," he said, switching on his torch and look-ing round. "We can make the opening bigger by pulling away some of those overhanging tufts of roots, and burrowing down in the sand below. It will be rather fun lying in the cave and squinting out through that narrow opening at the sea."

"We've got a very fine view," said Mary, and she lay down to peep out. "I can see the *Andy* from here. Jill's still sitting on deck. And look, you can see the Cliff of Birds too—over there in the distance—and make out the channel between the two ridges of rocks."

"We could see anyone coming to rescue us!" said Tom. "Couldn't we, Andy? We could easily see your father's boat from here. We could signal!"

There was a rocky ledge at one side of the cave. Mary patted it. "This will do to put our stores on," she said. "And we'll put our cushions and rugs on the sandy floor. We shall be very snug here. It would be great fun—if only Mother wouldn't be worried about us!"

"This cave will do fine," said Andy. "We'll go back and get our stores. Come on, Tom—squeeze out."

They all squeezed out. Andy looked up at the top edge of the entrance. He began to pull away some of the earth and roots that hung down from above. Soon he had made the entrance a little bigger.

"That will let more air in," he said. "It might be stuffy at night with four of us in. But it will certainly be warm! No wind can get in here to make us shiver and shake!"

They went back to the boat, pleased that they had found somewhere fairly near. They told Jill all about it. She showed them her ankle.

"It's *much* better!" she said. "It feels almost all right now. I could help to carry the things up."

"No, you can't," said Andy. "You rest it as much as you can. We'll take the things up, and leave you in charge of the boat whilst we go to and fro."

They went down into the cabin. They collected all the food—and there was quite a lot! What a good thing they had stocked the *Andy* so well!

They staggered off with the food. Jill got the little oil-stove ready for them to take too. They would need to boil water for tea or cocoa. She put the kettle ready to be taken.

It was very tiring work carrying the things over the rocks up to the cave. There were so many things to take. Andy did not mean to let anything be lost, if the boat were sunk. He meant to save all he could.

Rugs, cushions, fishing-tackle, the cabin lamp, mugs, plates, everything was stripped from the fishing-boat. The girls, not knowing that the boys were afraid that the boat might be scuttled, were astonished to see everything being taken. Mary thought it was most unnecessary work.

"Why do we take so much?" she grumbled. "I'm tired now! Andy, it's silly to take *every*thing!"

"Do as your skipper tells you!" said Tom.

"You're a good one to talk!" snapped Mary. "It was you who disobeyed Andy and got into a mess."

"You're tired, Mary," said Andy. "Stop carrying the things and let me finish them. Go back to Jill and see if you can help her part of the way up. Her foot is so much better that I believe she can manage with just your help."

By tea-time the cave was well stocked. Mary arranged the food on the rocky ledge there. "That's our larder," she told the boys. "And this bit is the dresser, with the plates and mugs and things. At the back here is the kitchen, because that's where we've put the stove and the kettle and saucepan. The other part is a bed-sitting-room, because we shall have to live there and sleep there too!"

When Jill came up to the cave, helped by Mary, she was delighted. She thought it all looked most exciting. The only thing was that it was rather dark there, and Andy did not want to use their torches too much, because of wearing out the batteries.

"We could light the cabin lamp," said Jill.

"There's not a great deal of oil," said Andy. "We'll only light that when it's really dark—at night. We can just manage to see inside the cave, if nobody stops up the entrance with his body! Tom, get out of the way. You're blocking our daylight!"

"I was just having a look-see," said Tom. "We've got the *Andy* under our eye all right here. If anyone tries any little tricks, we can see them."

"I suppose your father will rescue us to-morrow," said Jill. "We shall only have a night here. It's a pity really, because it's such fun to sleep in a cave, and keep having picnics."

"Do you suppose the people on this island—the ones who took our sail and oars, and flash those lights at the top—do you suppose they know we've come to this cave?" said Mary.

"I expect so," said Andy. "I've no doubt they've got look-outs posted, who see any ship, and can watch anyone's actions. They must have seen us there early this morning, down in the cove, and been very surprised. They couldn't have seen us coming last night—it was too dark."

"How annoyed they must have been, to see our boat there," said Tom. "We've butted in at just the wrong time for them. I guess they were jolly glad when they saw we were only children."

Jill and Mary were now getting tea. They wondered what to do for water to boil.

"Easy!" said Tom. "There is plenty of rain-water in the hollows of the rocks up here—left from last week's rain-storms, I should think. I'll fill your kettle for you, from one of the pools."

"Right," said Mary, and handed over the kettle. Tom squeezed out of the cave, found a good pool of rain-water quite nearby, and filled the kettle. Soon it was boiling on the oil-stove, making a nice gurgling sound. Jill cut some bread and butter, and put out a jar of plum jam.

"We'd better not have tins of meat or sardines, had we?" she said to Andy. "Just in case we aren't rescued to-morrow, and have to go on living here. We'll want the sardines and meat for dinner then."

"Yes," said Andy. "We must go slow on the food till we see what's going to happen. Anyway, this is a very nice tea. I like plum jam. I expect poor old Tom could eat a whole loaf, but he'll have to be content with a few slices! Have you got tinned milk for tea, Jill, or did we finish it all?"

"No. I've got plenty," said Jill. "As a matter of fact, we like spreading it on bread and butter like jam, so I brought quite a lot of tins. We shall be all right for tea and cocoa. Pass your mug, Andy. I'll fill it."

Even Andy, worried as he was about what might happen to his beloved boat, couldn't help enjoying his tea up there in the cave. But soon the cave felt very hot, because the oil-stove warmed it, and the children went and sat out on the ledge in the sunshine. It was a very beautiful view spreading before them.

"Rocks—and sea—and more rocks—and more sea— and sky and clouds and birds making a pattern in the air," said Jill, munching her slice of bread and jam. "I like looking at things like that when I'm having a picnic. It makes my bread and jam taste nicer!"

"Things always taste better when you eat them out of doors," said Mary. "I've often noticed that."

"Look!" said Andy suddenly. "Is that someone coming round the left-hand side of the cove down there? See— where that big rock sticks up. Yes—he's going to the *Andy*. Let's get back into the cave and watch. If he doesn't know where we are, we've no need to show ourselves!"

With beating hearts the children squeezed into the cave. They lay flat on their tummies and peered down to the cove below. They could see a man—he looked like a fisherman, and had big sea-boots on.

"He's going to the *Andy*," whispered Tom. "What's he going to do?"

The Hunt for the Children

HARDLY breathing, the four children watched the man walking over the rocks towards the *Andy*. He was a tall, burly man, very dark, and with a black beard.

"Do you know him, Andy?" whispered Tom. Andy shook his head.

"No. He doesn't come from our district. Look—he's getting into the boat."

A faint shout came up to the children. "He's shouting to us to come out!" said Mary. "He thinks we're still there!"

The man stood on the deck, waiting. But when no one answered him, or came up from below, he went to the cabin hatch and opened it. He looked down and saw no one there. He also saw that the boat looked remarkably empty of goods as well as of crew!

"He's found out that we've removed all our things from the boat!" said Andy.

The man went down into the cabin. Then he came up again, stood on the deck, and looked all about, as if he expected to be able to see the children somewhere.

"Look—there's another man now," whispered Tom. "See—coming round the cove where the first one came. What a funny little man!"

He was. He was bandy-legged, and walked as though he sat on a horse. He had on sea-boots and a sou'wester, and a black oil-skin that flapped in the wind. He was short and squat, and he yelled to the other man as he came. His voice came faintly on the wind to the children.

"Now they're talking together about our disappearance," said Tom, quite enjoying himself. "Do you think they'll come to find us, Andy? We're well hidden here."

The men talked together. The little bandy-legged one had a look round the boat and peered down into the cabin. It made Andy go red with rage to see strangers on his boat. He longed to go down and turn them off!

But if he did that he would give away the hiding-place. So he lay still, red to his ears, and Jill put her arm over his shoulder to comfort him. She knew what he was feeling. Andy was so proud of his boat, and loved her so much.

The men separated and went off in different directions. It was plain that they were hunting for the hidden children. They peeped about down in the cove, and occasionally shouted, though the children couldn't hear the words.

"Shouting to us to come out, I suppose," said Tom. "As if we would! I bet they don't find us!"

The men came up a bit higher, and looked all about the rocks there. There were one or two places there where the children might have hidden.

Now they could hear what the men shouted to one another. "Where are those brats?" yelled the bandy-legged man. "Wait till I find them! Wasting my time like this!"

The children lay quite quiet. They didn't like the look of the bandy-legged man at all as he came nearer. He had bushy eyebrows that almost hid his eyes, and a scar went all the way down one cheek. The dark man was good-looking, and spoke with a foreign accent. He looked stern as he went about the hunt.

"We'd better wriggle back right into the cave," said Andy. "If they come any higher they might just catch sight of us."

So they wriggled back. Soon they were crouching right at the very back, catching a glimpse of the distant sea through the narrow entrance. They kept very quiet, for they heard the sound of the men's climbing feet coming near.

"There's a cave somewhere about here!" they heard the bandy-legged man call. "I remember my dog going into it once. Maybe they've gone there."

"We will look," said the dark man, and his steps came nearer. The children saw his feet walking past the entrance! Their hearts almost stopped beating with fright. But the feet went right past and out of sight. Good!

Then they saw the bandy legs of the other man going by too. But just as he was passing, the legs stopped.

"I'm sure that cave was here," said his rather hoarse voice. "Wait—what's this!" His foot kicked into the entrance of the cave. Then he bent down and looked inside, finding it very awkward indeed. But he could see nothing, of course, for it was pitch-black inside the cave.

Jill gave a gulp of fright. Tom dug his fingers into her at once, to stop her. Surely she wasn't going to give them away! Jill put her hand over her mouth. She really hadn't been able to help giving that gulp.

"They cannot be in there," said the nearby voice of the dark man. "No one surely could creep in there! Look, there is a cave higher up. Maybe they are in that."

To the children's enormous relief the bandy-legged man moved on. They breathed more easily, but did not dare to move. They heard more shouting and calling and then there was silence.

"Is it safe to peep out?" said Tom, who was longing to know what was happening.

"No," said Andy. "They may be sitting quietly somewhere waiting for us to show ourselves. Keep still, Tom."

They all kept very still and quiet, only moving when their arms or legs felt cramped. Then they heard the voices again. The dark man sounded thoroughly impatient and exasperated.

"I tell you, Bandy, it is important that we find these children. If anyone comes to look for them they will signal to them—and they know too much! We must find them. It is impossible that they should have hidden themselves away so well."

"You can see for yourself they aren't here," said the other, sounding sulky. "They've taken all their things and maybe gone to the other side."

"I hope not!" said the other man. "They will fall into trouble there! No—they have not gone far, Bandy. They could not carry so many things very far."

The men were standing near the cave again now. The children heard the dark man suddenly give an exclamation.

"Look!" he said. "What's this? Spots of oil! Who could have spilt oil here but those children? They took the lamp out of the cabin—and the little cooking-stove, for it wasn't there. So maybe it was oil from one of those."

"Blow!" said Andy, between his teeth. He remembered how he had tipped the stove a little, bringing it to the cave over a rather difficult rock nearby.

"It looks as if they must be in that cave then, after all!" said the bandy man. "Yes, that's oil all right. Little pests, to give us so much trouble. I'll strike a match and look in the cave."

"He'll see us now," whispered Andy. "Now you leave everything to me, you others. I'll manage this."

Soon the bandy legs were to be seen outside the cave entrance once more. Then the man knelt down and looked with difficulty into the low, ground-level entrance. He struck a match, and held its flame inside the entrance. He gave a loud cry.

"Hey! Here they are, the whole boiling of them, lying as quiet as mice in a nest! Come on out, all of you!"

The children said nothing. The match went out. The man lit another and this time the dark man knelt down and looked into the entrance, his head almost on the ground. He saw the children too. He spoke to them with authority.

"Now, come out! We shan't hurt you, but we want to see you out of here. Come along."

"We're not coming," said Andy.

There was a silence. Then the bandy man began to lose his temper. He spluttered a little, and began to yell. "Look here, you, you . . ."

"That's enough, Bandy," said the dark man. He called into the cave.

"How many of you are there?"

"Four," said Andy. "And let me warn you that the first man who wriggles in here will get a blow on the head with the stove!"

"That's no way to talk," said the dark man after a moment's pause. "We're not going to hurt you. We want to take you somewhere much more comfortable."

"We couldn't be more comfortable than we are, thanks," said Andy politely.

"Are you coming or have I got to come in and get you!" yelled Bandy suddenly.

"Come in, if you like," said Andy. "If you come in feet

first we'll send you out double-quick, with a good shove. And if you come in head first, we're sorry for you. We've got the oil-stove waiting!"

"Leave them, Bandy," said the dark man, standing up. "Little idiots! It will be the worse for them when they do come out. We can always get them out when we want to."

"How?" asked Bandy.

"Easy enough. You'll see!" said the other. The children wondered what he meant.

"Well, we'll want them out as soon as we sight anything," said Bandy, standing up too. "Better give me your orders, chief!"

"We can leave them for tonight," said the dark man, and began to walk away. "We have other things we can do!"

Soon there was silence again. It was getting darker in the cave now, for the sun had gone, and twilight was coming. The children lay quite quiet for some time, but could hear nothing. Finally Andy crawled to the entrance and peered out.

"Can't see down into the cove," he said. "Too dark. Can't see any sign of those men, either. Beasts! How do they suppose we're going to be got out of here?"

"You wouldn't really drop the oil-stove on that man's head, would you?" asked Jill, very horrified at the thought.

" No," said Andy. "But I thought the threat might keep them out of here till to-morrow, when I hope my Dad will come with Uncle Ned and his boat. Then we'll creep out and yell for all we're worth!"

"That's what those men were afraid we'll do," said Tom. He yawned. "I feel sleepy. One of us will have to be on guard during the night, Andy. We don't want anyone creeping in to surprise us."

"Jill and I will take our turns to-night," said Mary. "You two boys hadn't much sleep last night. Can't we rig up a pile of tins at the entrance, so that anyone trying to creep in would knock them over, and warn the one on guard?"

"Jolly good idea, Mary," said Andy. "We'll do that at once. I feel as sleepy as Tom does. You can have the first watch, me the next, Jill the next, and Tom the next. Where are the tins? I can't see in this darkness!"

Mary lighted the lamp, and the cave at once glowed into warm yellow light. It seemed cosy and snug in there. The children wrapped their rugs round them and put cushions at their heads. Mary sat bolt upright, proud to have the first watch. She had built up a pile of tins at the entrance to the cave. Now no one could get in without being heard at once.

Andy blew out the lamp. Darkness settled on the cave once more. Jill put out her hand and took Mary's. "I'll hold your hand just to keep you company whilst you're watching," she whispered. "Good night!"

Soon there was silence in the cave except for the peaceful breathing of three sleeping children. Mary sat tense, holding her breath at every sound. She did hope that nobody would come whilst she was keeping watch!

Plenty of Things Happen!

MARY watched and listened until it was time to wake Andy. She felt quite worn out by the time she had been on guard for two hours. They were each keeping guard for the same time—two hours. But it seemed a very long time, when everything was dark and still.

Andy had nothing to report when he woke Jill. Jill kept watch for two hours, feeling rather sleepy at times but keeping herself awake by reciting softly all the poetry she had ever learnt.

Tom's turn came next. He was very difficult to wake, as usual. Jill thought she never would wake him! But at last she had him sitting up, rubbing his eyes.

"You're to wake Andy in two hours' time, and he'll take the dawn watch," she said. "He says he doesn't mind, he'll have had plenty of sleep by then."

Tom couldn't keep his eyes open! He rubbed them and nearly yawned his head off. Then he felt hungry and wondered where the girls had put the chocolate. He felt about for Andy's torch and found it. He switched it on and flashed the light on to the little ledge where the food was stored.

Andy was awake immediately the torch flashed on. He sat upright with a jerk, blinking.

"What's up?" he said.

"Nothing!" whispered Tom. "I only wanted some chocolate. I'll never keep awake unless I have something to eat. Lie down. I'll wake you when it's your turn again."

He saw the chocolate piled at the end of the ledge. He took a bar, snapped off the torch, and began to tear the paper off the chocolate. Andy lay down with a grunt and was soon sleeping soundly again.

Nothing happened in Tom's watch. He woke Andy just before dawn. The boy sat up, and saw the first grey light filtering in through the low cave-entrance. He wriggled there and looked out. He could see nothing at all.

When the sun rose the others awoke. Jill sat up, stretching. She knew where she was at once, but Mary couldn't imagine.

"Where am I?" she said, sitting up, half-frightened.

"Only in the cave, silly," said Jill. "It's daylight again. Golly, I feel stiff. I'm a bit cold too. I vote we get the stove going and boil some water for cocoa."

Tom was wriggling to the cave entrance to have a breath of fresh air. He sniffed eagerly, and looked down to the cove below. He gave such a loud cry that everyone jumped, and Mary dropped the match she was about to strike.

"What's up? What's the matter?" they cried.

"Our boat—it's gone. It isn't there!" cried Tom. "Look! The cove's quite empty. No boat there at all!"

All four looked down to the cove below. It was just as Tom had said. The boat was gone. The *Andy* was no longer there.

Andy looked very miserable. He didn't say anything at all. Tom knew how he was feeling.

"Oh, Andy, you don't think those men have sunk her, do you?" he said in a hushed voice. "Surely nobody could do such a wicked thing to a beautiful boat like that!"

Andy still said nothing. He left the others and went to the back of the cave, where he busied himself lighting the stove and putting the kettle on to boil. He couldn't bear to think that his lovely boat might be lying far down at the bottom of the water.

"Poor Andy!" whispered Jill, with tears in her eyes. "Isn't it awful? Tom, why should those men sink our boat?"

"I suppose so that no one should see it and guess we were here, if they came to look for us," said Tom, feeling that the girls ought to know how serious things were. "You see, we have stumbled on some kind of secret, and those men don't want us to tell anyone. But they know someone will be sure to come hunting for us, so they've sunk our boat, and mean to hide us away somewhere, so that we can't be found—then we shan't be able to tell what little we know!"

The girls looked scared. Then Jill cheered up. "But they

haven't taken us anywhere, and when we see Andy's father's boat coming, we'll all climb up on to the high rocks above the cave and signal. I'll take off my vest and wave it!"

"Kettle's boiling," came Andy's voice from the back. "Going to make the cocoa, Jill?"

Jill scrambled back. Her foot was practically all right again. But she blamed herself very much for her accident, for if she had not twisted her ankle, they might all by now have been safely back at home. So she was eager to please Andy in every way and show him how sorry she was.

Andy looked very miserable. Jill didn't say anything to him, but she gave his arm a quick squeeze. She too felt very gloomy when she thought of the beautiful boat lying on the bottom of the sea—but she knew that to Andy his boat meant much more than a lovely plaything. That was all it really was to the three visitors, but to Andy the boat was a friend and a comrade.

"Dad ought to be along soon," said Andy, as they ate their breakfast. "When we didn't come home last night, as we should have done, everyone would get the wind up and be worried. Dad would start out for the Cliff of Birds early this morning. If he didn't find us there he'd come along here. We must keep a look-out."

They finished breakfast. Andy peered out of the cave. "I must just slip down to the cove and have a look to see if the poor old *Andy* is at the bottom there," he said. "I won't be long. And I won't be caught, so don't be afraid. But I've just *got* to go and have a look. Keep a watch out, Tom."

The boy wriggled out of the cave, and the others saw him running and skipping like a goat, down the steep rocks that sloped to the cove. They saw him standing where the *Andy* had been anchored, peering down into the water here and there.

"Poor old Andy. This has upset him," said Jill. "It's awful to lose his boat like that. I feel it's all my fault too."

"Look—there's that bandy man again!" said Tom, suddenly. "And two others with him! They've seen Andy—but he's seen them too. Look at him leaping up the rocks! Oh, Andy, hurry, hurry!"

Andy was not afraid of being caught by the three men. He was far swifter than they were. They yelled at him and ran, but they were no match at all for the boy. He leapt up the rocks, and came panting to the cave. He wriggled in with plenty of time to spare.

"I don't know if they've come for us," he panted. "But they won't make us come out! I don't see how they can unless they like to risk wriggling in on their tummies—and they are at our mercy then!"

"Andy, did you see the boat?" asked Jill anxiously. Andy shook his head.

"No—they haven't sunk her just there. I think they must have taken her out to sea a bit and scuttled her in really deep water. There's no sign of her down there."

"I suppose they thought your father might spot her, lying in the cove at the bottom," said Tom. "They must have taken her out in the night. And not one of us heard a thing!"

"Well, the cove is a good way off," said Andy, getting back his breath. "Now look out—here come the men."

There was the dark man with the beard; the bandy-legged man—and one that Tom recognized at once.

"Look—see the fisherman with the glasses on his nose? Well, that's one of the men I saw in the cave at the Cliff of Birds! How did he get here? Did the motor-boat call for him and take him off?"

"He's not the one with hairy legs, is he—the man whose legs we saw when he sat above us on the Cliff of Birds?" asked Jill.

"No. He's not here," said Tom. "Nasty-looking collection, aren't they?"

Andy felt desperate. He was angered by the disappearance of his boat, and quite ready to push any of the men down the rocks, if only he could! He was anxious, too, for the girls. Their mother had put them into his charge—and here they were in the midst of danger. Andy was quite determined to fight with any weapon he could, if the men tried to wriggle into the cave.

The three came to the cave. The dark man called out to them. "Well, children, are you more sensible this morning? Are you coming out? I advise you to."

No one said anything. The man called again, impatiently. "Come along now! No one will hurt you! You'll be sorry if you don't come out of your own free will. We don't want to *make* you come!"

Still no reply. There was a short silence, and the dark man gave a rapid order.

"Set it going, Bandy."

Bandy set something down by the cave, just within the entrance. It looked like some sort of can. The children couldn't quite make out what it was. They watched in silence.

Bandy struck a match and held it to something in the can. It flared up. Bandy seemed to damp it down and, instead of flames, smoke came out.

The wind was blowing in their direction and it blew the thick, billowing smoke into the cave. Tom got a smell of it first and he coughed.

"The beasts!" said Andy suddenly. "They're trying to smoke us out of the cave—like hunters smoke out wild animals!"

The smoke poured in. The children began to cough. They choked. The smoke was thick and smelt horrid and bitter. It was quite harmless, but the children didn't know that. They felt frightened.

"We'll have to go out," spluttered Andy. "It's no good. We'll have to go. Keep close to me when we're out, girls, and do exactly what I say. Don't be afraid. I don't think for a minute we'll come to any harm."

Before he went out, Andy felt along the ledges for the packet of salt he knew was there. The others didn't see him and would have been surprised if they had. Andy tore open the packet, and slipped the salt into his pocket. He had a little plan for that salt!

Then, panting and coughing, he crawled out of the cave. The girls came next, and then Tom. The men stared at them.

"Why, they're only kids—except for this fisher-boy," said Bandy. "Interfering little varmints."

"Look! Look, Andy! There's your father's boat!" suddenly cried Tom, and they all swung round. Sure enough, away in the distance was a big fishing-boat, the one used by Andy's uncle and his father when they wanted a bigger boat than Andy's.

"Hurrah!" yelled Tom. "We're all right. You'll have to let us go now! There's Andy's father."

"Come on. Take them away," said the dark man. "There's no time to be lost. Blindfold them!"

To the children's great dismay they were each blindfolded with big red handkerchiefs. Where were they going? And why were their eyes bandaged? Were they going to some secret hide-out that no one must know the way to?

The men pushed them forward roughly, and they stumbled over a rocky path, not seeing where they went.

"Oh," wept Mary, "let us wait! Let us wait for Andy's father! We'll go home then. Let us go, please let us go!"

But the men pushed them on, and when Andy's father sailed into the cove, there was no one to be seen!

Prisoners!

THE four children were pushed along by the men. They were afraid of falling, but the men guided them over the rough places. It seemed to them all as if they were going upwards, not on the level. How they hoped that Andy's father would spot them, if only he had his field-glasses!

Andy was doing his best to try and memorize the way, as they went along. "Up all the time—to the left first and then fairly straight—then a steep bit up, where they had to help us—then to the left again, keeping inwards. I suppose we are behind big rocks now, so that no one can see us from the sea."

Andy was doing something else too, that he hoped his captors were not noticing! He was dropping little pinches of salt here and there as he went! He had made a hole in his pocket, and he let out a bit of the salt every now and again.

He wanted to be able to find his way to the smugglers' hiding-place, if ever he got free and had the chance to! He hoped that he might be able to follow the little trail of salt he was leaving!

"If only it doesn't rain!" thought the boy. "If it rains, the salt will melt and there won't be any sign of it. Well, I must hope for the best."

After about ten minutes' rough stumbling, the men told the children to halt. There was a pause. Andy strained his eyes, and then tried to pull off his bandage. But he got a hard clip on the ear at once.

He heard a grating noise that puzzled him. Then the children were pushed roughly forward again, and it seemed darker, through their bandages.

"Going into the island itself—a cave of some sort, or a passage," thought Andy, as the men pushed the children along again. They went upwards again, and Andy cautiously put his hands out to the side of him. He felt rocky walls each side. Yes, they were in a passage inside the island!

At last they all came to a stop. "You'll be safe here for a bit!" said the jeering voice of the bandy-legged man, and he stripped off the red handkerchiefs that bound their eyes.

They blinked. They were standing in a high-roofed place, looking at a big door. Andy felt something bright at the back of him and swung round. He gave a gasp.

They were in a cave, very high up, that opened on to the sunlit sea. It lay very far below, moving slowly. There was an absolutely sheer drop down from the cave to the sea—a very frightening drop!

There was a bang, as the heavy wooden door behind them shut. The children heard bolts being shot into place. They were prisoners—but what a strange prison!

"It's a big cave, with a door at the back—and a terribly steep drop down outside," said Jill, peeping out and drawing back very quickly. "Goodness—I shan't look out again like that. It makes me feel awfully giddy. We couldn't possibly get out that way."

"Can we see Andy's father's boat?" asked Tom, almost dazzled by the brightness outside, after having his eyes bandaged for so long.

They all gazed out earnestly. But there was nothing to be seen at all except a dangerous, treacherous, rock-strewn shore, where waves battered themselves into foam and spray.

"It's said that no one can get beyond a certain point in a boat, if they want to sail round the island," said Andy. "I don't believe anyone ever *has* sailed right round it. You can't get near the other side—it's too dangerous. We must be almost on the other side now, I should think. I doubt if my father could get round as far as this."

"I bet those men knew that then," said Tom gloomily. "They knew that we couldn't possibly signal from here, because we wouldn't see your father's boat. Beasts!"

"I hope they're not going to keep us here long," said Andy. "I don't fancy being shut up like this, without any food or rugs or anything."

"This is as bad as last year's adventure," said Jill. "Well —almost as bad!"

The four children sat down in the cave. Andy got up after a while and went to the door. He tried it, but, of course, it was fast shut.

"I knew it would be. But I thought I'd just try," said Andy. "I do wonder how long they'll keep us here— till my father's gone home again, I suppose! And I do wonder too where they sank the poor old *Andy*. I hate to think of her at the bottom of the sea."

"With fish swimming in the cabins, and crabs getting into the bunks," said Jill. "Horrid!"

For about three hours nothing happened. The children gazed out to sea, hoping against hope to see a boat or a ship they could signal to. But not one came into sight. Only the gulls circled and glided nearby, calling to one another in their loud voices. The children watched them, for they had nothing else to do.

Then there came the sound of the door being unbolted. They all sat up at once. Who was it?

It was Bandy. He came in, carrying a big jug of water and a plate of bread and meat. Nothing else at all.

"You don't deserve a thing!" he said in his rather hoarse voice. "Interfering, tiresome nuisances you are! Eat this, and be glad of it!"

"Bandy! How long are we to be kept here?" asked Andy. "And what have you done with my boat? Sunk her?"

"Why? Are you thinking of trying to sail away in her?" asked Bandy, with a nasty smile. "You can give up all hope of that! She's sunk all right!"

Andy turned away, sick at heart. He had hoped against hope that his lovely boat wasn't really sunk.

"Can't you let us out now?" asked Tom. "I suppose you shut us up because Andy's father came. Cowards!"

"Do you want a clip on the ear?" said Bandy, coming into the cave and glaring at Tom.

"Shut up, Tom, now," said Andy. "It's no good provoking him. It's pretty boring here, Bandy. Can't we have something to do? And the rock is very hard to sit on."

"Serves you right. Children that come sticking their noses into what isn't their business deserve all they get," said Bandy, who seemed to enjoy being nasty. "Maybe

93

you'll be here for weeks! Ha ha—how do you like the thought of that?"

"I think, Bandy, if you do a thing like that, you'll be very sorry for yourself later on, when all this is known," said Andy in a quiet voice. "You'll be severely punished."

"Bah!" said Bandy rudely, and went out and shut the door, bolting it noisily. "Bah!" they heard him say again outside.

The food made them feel a little better, though the bread was very stale and hard, and the meat tasted a bit musty. But they did not feel very cheerful as they gazed out through the opening at the sea and the sky, thinking that they might be there for weeks.

Jill and Mary looked so upset that Andy tried to cheer them up. "He was only being beastly," he told them. "Just trying to scare us all. He'll let us out as soon as my father's boat has gone away. Don't you worry, girls!"

They saw no sign of Andy's father that day. They did not know how he and Andy's uncle sailed up and down, and round about, looking for the missing boat and the children. They did not see them sailing to the Cliff of Birds and anchoring there to climb the cliff. Nor did they see them come back again and again to Smuggler's Rock, hunting for a cove where they might see the *Andy*.

Towards five o'clock, when they were all feeling very hungry indeed, they heard the bolts of the door being pulled back. This time it was the dark man who came in. He spoke to them in his deep voice, and they heard again his slightly foreign accent and knew that he was not English.

"You can go now. The ship that has been hunting for you has given you up, and has gone. But I warn you that if it is sighted again, you will once more have to come here to this cave, where you will be imprisoned until the boat has once again gone."

"We shall have to be set free of the island some time," said Andy. "Why all this mystery and fuss? What are you doing that you want to hide?"

"Children shouldn't ask dangerous questions!" said the man, and his eyes gleamed angrily. "When we have finished here, you shall go, but not till then. You will now be blindfolded once again and taken down to the rocks you know."

So, once again, the red handkerchiefs were tied tightly round the children's eyes, and Bandy and the dark man took them out of the cave. Downwards they went, and then came out into the open air. They were taken some way farther over the rocks, and then the bandages were stripped off their eyes.

They blinked. "We're near the cove!" said Tom. "Good. Let's go up to our cave and get a meal. I'm jolly hungry."

Andy watched to see which way the men went. They rounded a corner of steep rocks and were soon out of sight. "If only I knew where they went and what they do!" he said, in a low voice. "What *is* going on here? Well—I'll find the way into the heart of the island, and discover what's going on before I'm much older!"

"But how can you?" said Tom. "We were blindfolded. We'd never find the way."

"I'm going to look for it," said Andy, "but not till we've had something to eat. I want those men to get well out of the way first!"

They went to their cave. It seemed almost like coming home, to squeeze in at the narrow entrance! Jill and Mary were full of delight to be there again. They looked at their larder hungrily.

"What shall we have? I think we'll go a splash, and have something good," said Jill. "What about a tin of tongue—and shall we hot up a tin of peas to go with it? We've got just one. And have a tin of pine-apple chunks afterwards?"

"With condensed milk," said Mary. "And we'll make cocoa too—lots of it."

"Well, for goodness' sake hurry up about it," said Tom. "I'm hungrier than ever when I hear you talk like that!"

They had a most delicious meal, and ate every single thing they had prepared for it, and drank the last drop from the cocoa jug. As Mary put back the mugs, she missed the packet of salt.

"Where's the salt gone?" she said in surprise.

"I took it!" said Andy. "And I'll tell you why! I made a hole in my pocket, and as we went blindfolded on our way this morning, I kept dropping out pinches of salt

—so, you see, I ought to be able to find the way into the depths of the island, by following my trail of salt!"

"Oh, Andy—what a *marvellous* idea!" said Tom. "Let's go now and see if we can find the trail. Come on, do let's! I do think that was a clever thing to do! We'll go and spy on those men this very evening!"

A Trail to Follow

TOM, Jill and Mary thought it was very exciting to have a salt trail to follow.

"Now we'll be able to get inside the island, and see what the men are doing," said Mary, squeezing out of the cave entrance. "Come on. Let's all go now. My goodness, we'd better hurry! Look at those black clouds."

Andy looked at them in alarm. They were rain-clouds. "Blow, blow, blow!" he said.

"Are you talking to the wind, or just being annoyed?" asked Jill.

"I'm being annoyed," said Andy, as he felt the first drop of rain on his cheek. "The rain will melt all my trail of salt! Isn't that enough to make anyone annoyed?"

"Well, let's buck up then, before it begins to pour!" said Tom, and they scuttled down the rocks. They found a pinch of salt on a rock, and exclaimed at it.

"Here's one! We passed by here. And there's another! Come on, we can easily spot the white grains!"

They followed the salt trail for a little way up the rocks, and round to the left. Then the rain came down properly, and in a trice the salt had disappeared! Andy looked very gloomy.

"Just my luck! Why didn't I follow the trail straight-away, without stopping to have a meal? And why didn't I think of something more sensible than salt? But I was in such a hurry. and it was the only thing that came into my mind. Blow!"

"Never mind. Andy," said Jill. "It was an awfully good idea. I'd never have thought of it at all!"

"Well—couldn't we do it again, if those men take us off to the high-up cave another time?" asked Tom. "I bet your father won't give up hunting for us yet, Andy.

D

I bet he'll be along again to-morrow. If so, those men will shut us up again. Bandy said they would."

"Yes. There's a chance Dad might sail this way again to-morrow," said Andy. "He might even bring out some of his friends, in their boats, to search all round. We could try out my idea again."

"But not with salt," said Jill. "That's too easy to melt—or it might be blown away if it falls in a wind-swept place. Let's think of something else."

"It must be something the men don't notice," said Mary. "What can it be?"

Nobody could think of anything for some time. Then Tom had a brain-wave. "I know! Do you remember seeing those little pink shells down in the cove? Well, what about gathering up those, filling our pockets with them? No one would notice shells here and there—they're so usual by the sea. We could all drop one now and again as we go, and there would be a lovely trail to follow!"

"Yes—and one that wouldn't melt away if it rained!" said Jill.

"Good idea, young Tom," said Andy. "We'll do that. We could collect them now—then we'd have them ready in case the men took us off to that cave again to-morrow."

So they all hunted for the little pink shells in the cove, and found dozens of them. They put them into their pockets. It wouldn't matter in the least if the men searched their pockets and found the shells—because children always did collect them. Tom felt very pleased with his idea.

It grew dark. "Better go back to our cave," said Andy. "We'll light the lamp and have a cosy evening. It's rather cold now too. We got a bit wet in that squall of rain, though it didn't last long. It will be nice to be warm and dry—and we'll make some tea and have biscuits for supper—if Tom hasn't eaten them all yet!"

"Of course I haven't!" said Tom indignantly. "I've had just the same number as you!"

They went up to their cave and squeezed in. Andy lighted the lamp, and the stove too, so that they could boil the kettle. He had filled it with rain-water, which most conveniently lay in a nearby hollow, not far from the cave.

The cave certainly looked very cosy, and was soon

warm and stuffy. But the children didn't mind that, for they were cold and wet.

"This is nice," said Jill, pulling a rug round her. "I know horrid things have happened, and I hate to think of people being worried about us—but I can't help enjoying being in this cosy cave, and feeling warm and dry, and having ginger biscuits to nibble."

Everyone felt the same, though Andy looked rather stern and thoughtful. Jill knew he was always thinking of his lost boat. He seemed to have lost his ready smiles and jokes now. She gave him an extra biscuit because she felt sorry for him.

They slept well that night in the cave, and no one kept watch, because there didn't seem to be any need to. They didn't feel that the men would really harm them, and they all wanted a good night's sleep.

So they slept soundly, and nothing disturbed them. They woke when the sun was quite high, and Andy was surprised. "We're late this morning!" he said. "I'm going to rinse my face and hands in that pool over there—I feel messy."

They all did the same. Jill produced a comb and they made their hair tidy. They had begun to look like little savages, Mary said!

They had a rather poor breakfast of stale bread and butter and jam. But they did not like to open any more of their precious tins, in case the men were mean with food. They hadn't much liked the bread and meat they had had the day before.

"Andy! The men are coming again!" said Tom suddenly. He was sitting outside on the ledge. "And oh golly, look over there! One—two, three—four—*five* fishing-boats! My word, your father's got half the fleet out to look for us!"

"Let's signal, quick!" cried Andy. But the boats were too far away to see them, and at the same moment the men came up to the cave. They were the same three as before, with red handkerchiefs dangling ready in their hands to blindfold the children.

"Remember the shells," said Andy in a low voice.

"Come out, all of you," said the dark man's voice. Tom had scrambled back, so they were all in the cave now.

"We'll go out without making a fuss," said Andy to the

others. "We don't want to be smoked out again. That was horrid. I coughed all day and so did the rest of you."

They squeezed out of the cave and stood up. The men blindfolded them quickly. Then once more they were pushed along the rocks, and made their staggering, stumbling way as before. Again they went to the left, and upwards, and again they came to a standstill, and heard the curious grating sound.

Then they were pushed into a darker place and knew they were inside the rocky hill. Before long they were in the same cave as before, looking out to sea from a great height, and heard the wooden door being bolted behind them.

"I dropped my . . ." began Jill in an eager voice, and broke off with a groan as Tom and Andy gave her sharp digs with their fingers. "Don't! What did you do that for?"

Andy nodded his head towards the door. "You don't know if any of them are behind, listening to what we may say," he whispered. "Don't say a thing till I nod my head at you."

They all stayed silent for a while. Then, when Andy was certain their captors had gone, he nodded his head. "But speak low, all the same," he said.

"I dropped my shells all the way," whispered Jill. "I haven't a single one left! They just gave out when we got here!"

"I've dropped all mine too," said Mary. "I was so afraid the men would notice. Did you drop yours, Tom?"

"Of course," said Tom. "I kept *hearing* mine drop too, and thinking the men would notice."

"You've got very sharp ears," said Andy. "Nobody else would hear those tiny shells dropping! I've got about four left. I was afraid I'd drop them all before I came to the place, and that would be sickening!"

"Well, we seem to have done all right between us," said Tom in the same whisper that everyone was using. "We ought to be able to track down the trail here easily enough. We could get inside the hill then and snoop round and find out a lot!"

"I think we'll have to do it at night," said Andy. "The men will be about in the daytime—but at night I imagine they sleep—except the man who flashes that light at the top of the hill."

Blindfolded, they were pushed along

"Oooh—at night?" said Jill, rather scared. "I wouldn't like that!"

"Well, only Tom and I will go," said Andy. "We will leave you cosily asleep in the cave, and get back to you before dawn. We'll take your torches too—then we shall have plenty of light."

"I wonder if those fishing-boats are sailing all round and about, looking for signs of us everywhere," said Tom. "I wish we had left something about, so that if they landed on the island, they would see it, and know we were here."

"I'd thought of that," said Andy. "But you may be sure the men would remove every single thing that might tell we were here. Dad won't find anything. He'll have to go back again to-day, with all the others, and report that there's nothing to be found. I wish we could send some message to your mother. She'll be so anxious."

"Yes, she will," said Jill. "She'll never, never let us go out alone with you in a boat again, Andy! Last year we got wrecked in a storm, and had a tremendous adventure for weeks—and this year we've got caught by smugglers— if they *are* smugglers!"

"Well, we couldn't help it," said Andy. "How were we to know that there was all this going on in the Cliff of Birds and Smuggler's Rock?"

Once more dry bread and meat was presented to the children by Bandy. This time it was ham, which tasted a lot nicer. Then, sooner than the day before, they were set free. But they were blindfolded just the same, and led, stumbling and unsteady to the rocks above the cove.

"I think your friends will now give up the search for you!" said the dark man in rather a nasty voice. "So you will be free to roam on the island. But you will find that steep, sheer rocks make it impossible for you to get round to the other side, so do not try. You may fall and be hurt —and if so, we shall not help you."

"What kind people you are!" remarked Andy. Bandy looked as if he would like to box his ears, but he didn't. The men went off and left them alone.

Jill ran a little way up the rocks as soon as they were out of sight. She came back, her face pink with excitement.

"Our trail of shells is there, quite easy to see! You'll

102

be able to follow them well, Tom and Andy. They stretch up over the rocks," said Jill. "I can make out the trail for quite a long way! "

"Well, I hope the men don't spot it then," said Andy. "We'll do a bit of tracking to-night, Tom. It will be most exciting! "

A Queer Midnight Journey

THE boys thought they would not start following the trail
till about midnight. Then they could be fairly certain that
the men would be asleep. They decided to try and go to
sleep themselves for a few hours first, so that they would
not be too tired.

"I'll keep awake for you, and wake you at midnight, if
you like," said Jill. "I've got a watch. If I have the lamp
on, I know I shall keep awake."

"No. It's all right. I shall wake at midnight," said Andy,
who was one of the clever people able to wake himself
at any time he planned. "We can all go to sleep."

So they cuddled up in their rugs, put their heads down
on the cushions they had brought from the boats, and were
soon asleep and dreaming.

At midnight, just as he had said he would, Andy awoke.
He sat up and switched on his torch. Almost twelve
o'clock! He shook Tom hard and woke him.

"Oooh!" said Tom and woke with a jump.

"Sh! Don't wake the girls!" whispered Andy. "It's time
for us to go. Buck up!"

"Give me Jill's torch," whispered Tom. "You know
mine's no use. I must have a torch."

Andy handed him one. Then the boys squeezed out of
the cave and stood on the windy hill. It was cold and dark.
Clouds covered the night sky.

"Now to pick up the trail!" said Andy, and shone his
torch cautiously down, shading it with his fingers so as
not to show too much light.

They soon picked up the trail of pink shells which
gleamed brightly in the torch-light. The boys made their
way over the rocks, following the shells easily. There was
one bit where the trail broke, and they went wrong, but
they soon came back to the trail, and found the right way.

"We must all have stopped dropping shells at the same moment!" said Tom, thinking it was queer to find such a gap. "But it wasn't much of a gap. Come on."

They went on and on, round to the left and upwards. Then the trail of shells suddenly stopped.

"This is where we must have gone inside," said Andy and he shone his torch on the rocks that towered beside him just there. But there was no way in at all. The wall of rock stood there, unbroken. There was no entrance into the hill.

"Funny!" said Andy. "Perhaps the trail goes on after all. Perhaps we've come to a gap again, where none of us threw down shells! I'll go on and see. You stay here and shine your torch out now and again, so that I shall know where to come back to, if I can't find any more shells."

He soon came back. "There's no more to be seen," he said. "This *must* be where we went in. But how in the world can anyone walk through solid rock!"

He shone his torch on the rocky wall again. He discovered a crack of about an inch wide, that seemed to go inside the hill.

"Funny!" said Andy, and shone his torch up and down the crack. "Look, Tom—this crack seems the only way into the hill—but how could anyone squeeze through a crack like that? We certainly didn't!"

The boys tried to find some other place to get in, but there was none. They were forced to come back to the same place once more. Andy remembered something.

"Do you remember the funny noise we heard?" he asked Tom. "Sort of grating noise. I wonder if by any chance this rock moves—you know, like the stone moved in the Open Sesame cave in the tale of *Ali Baba and the Forty Thieves.*"

"But how could we move a heavy, rocky wall like that?" said Tom.

Andy went to the crack again. He shone his torch down it. Then he shone his torch above and below—and he found something on a ledge below that made him almost shout.

"Look, Tom—an iron bar! Put there to use as a lever, I shouldn't wonder! Well, I'll try!"

He picked up the strong iron bar, and slipped it into the crack. He and Tom pressed hard—and lo and behold, part of the rock slipped aside with a curious grating noise! It was evidently balanced so finely on its base that it could be moved almost at a touch. When it was open, the boys saw the dark entrance into the hill. Andy shone his torch in. It looked rather frightening.

"Well—who would have thought of a way in like that!" said Andy in a whisper. "I feel like Ali Baba now. Don't let's try and shut the rock behind us, in case we can't open it from the inside. We don't want to make ourselves prisoners."

They left the rock as it was, put down the iron bar and went inside the hill. A long tunnel yawned in front of them. After they had followed it for some way it split in two. One tunnel then went upwards and the other downwards. Which should they follow?

"Up, I think," said Andy. "The upgoing one may lead us to the light at the top of the island and we could have a good look at it."

The boys crept on up the tunnel, using their torches, but switching them off at once if they thought they heard anything. But the inside of the rocky hill was dark and silent. It was weird to be there in the middle of the night, not knowing what they might see or hear!

The tunnel split into two again. One tunnel ran on the level and the other still went up. Andy and Tom went along the level one to see what they could find. They came to a strong wooden door, with bolts and a lock.

"I bet this is the door of the cave those men shut us in to-day and yesterday," said Andy. "We'll see, shall we?"

Cautiously they opened the door. Yes—it was the very same cave. They retraced their steps and joined the tunnel that went on upwards.

They suddenly saw a light shining somewhere in front of them. "Quiet!" hissed Andy. "Stand still and listen."

But there was nothing at all to be heard. So they went cautiously on towards the light. They came into an enormous cave, lighted by a great ship's lantern that swung from an iron hook in the rocky roof. This cave was furnished most comfortably, with two or three mattresses, a table, chairs, and cupboards in which stores were evidently kept. A stove was burning, with a kettle boiling away on top.

On the table was set a meal—a very good meal too,

which made Tom feel very hungry indeed. The pink slices of ham lay on a dish, and a jar of tongue had been opened nearby. A rich dark plum-cake stood on a plate, and a tin of peaches had been opened.

"Look at that!" said Tom, his mouth watering, "I really *must* have a slice of that ham!"

"Be careful! The meal is set for someone and the kettle boiling, so that the man it's meant for can't be far away!" whispered Andy. "He'll be back soon. We don't want to be caught."

"Can't we just nip in and get some of the ham?" begged Tom. "There's time!"

"Well, quick then!" said Andy. He nipped in with Tom. The boys snatched four slices of the ham, and a half loaf of bread. Andy cut an enormous slice of the cake. They stuffed everything into their pockets. They were just about to run out of the cave into the tunnel when they heard someone coming!

The Someone sang as he came, a sea-shanty. It was Bandy's hoarse voice.

"Quick! Hide!" said Andy, looking round. "Into that chest, quick!"

They lifted the lid of an enormous chest and got inside it, putting the lid down quietly just as Bandy came into the lighted cave. He came in singing lustily, and took the kettle off the stove.

He made himself some tea, and then sat down to the table. He stared at the ham.

"Look at that! Where's half the ham gone? And where's my bread? If that greedy pig of a Stumpy has come in here and taken my supper again I'll knock him down!"

Bandy growled and muttered. Then he saw that someone had cut a huge slice of the plum-cake and he rose to his feet in anger.

"My cake too! I'll teach him! I'll box his ears till he can't tell if he's standing up or sitting down. I'll—I'll ..."

He disappeared out of the cave, taking the tunnel that led downwards. Andy and Tom badly wanted to laugh. Poor Stumpy! He would deny till he was black in the face that he had taken Bandy's supper, but Bandy wouldn't believe him.

"Let's get out of here whilst we've got the chance," said

Andy, walking out. "We'd better go on upwards, or we shall run into Bandy. Come on, Tom."

Tom stopped to snatch a few more bits of ham, and another piece of cake. Then he ran after Andy into the tunnel again. Upwards they went, wondering where they would come to.

They had to use their torches again. Presently there were rough steps cut in a steep upward passage. It seemed as if they were never coming to an end. Tom gave a huge pant and sat down.

"Andy, I *must* have a rest! I simply must! Those steps are so steep."

Andy sat down beside him, panting too. He switched off his torch. He smiled in the darkness to think of Bandy going off to accuse Stumpy, whoever he might be, of taking his supper. The ham, bread and cake were now safely disposed of, and both boys felt very satisfied.

They got up after a rest and continued on their way. Suddenly the steps stopped, and they came out on to a kind of platform. The wind swept suddenly and viciously on them.

"We're on the top of Smuggler's Rock, the very top—where that light was flashed from!" cried Andy. "My, isn't the wind fierce!"

"Look—here's the enormous lamp that must have flashed those signals!" said Tom, and he flashed his torch on to a great lamp, which was, of course, not now lighted. "See, Andy—the beams from this would flash a long way —to ships far out, waiting to come in with smuggled goods!"

"My word!" said Andy. "That's just about right! We're very high up here. Ships many miles away could catch these signals."

Suddenly he clutched Tom's arm. "Listen—aren't those footsteps—and whistling again? Perhaps Bandy is coming up to signal. Hop under the platform that the lamp's on. We may not be seen at all!"

They crept under the wooden platform on which the great lamp stood. Then Bandy came, and began to do something to the lamp. In a minute or two brilliant flashes lit up the night. The lamp was signalling to someone.

Bandy signalled for ten minutes. Then he turned out the light in some way and went down the steps again. The boys didn't dare to follow. They went down a few steps, found a rough, hidden corner in the rocky wall, and lay down there. In a few moments they were asleep!

They awoke at dawn, stiff and shivering, cross at having been to sleep. Andy went on to the windy platform and looked all round—what a perfectly marvellous view. Why, he could see all round the rocky island!

He looked down on the side he had never seen before, —and gave a low cry. "Look, Tom—look down there. Whatever do you make of that!"

More Discoveries

THE two boys gazed down, far, far down, to where the sea gleamed in the early sunlight. They saw a blue harbour, an almost round cove, protected on all sides by steep, rugged rocks. At first it seemed as if there was no outlet to the sea itself at all—the harbour looked more like an inland lake.

It was full of motor-boats, some large, some small! They lay at rest, all but one, which was just making its way cautiously into the cove, through so narrow an opening that the boys could scarcely make it out from where they were.

"Look at that!" said Andy. "Whoever would dream there was this cove, this natural harbour the other side of the island! No one can see it from the other side—and I imagine that unless you know your way among those far-flung rocks stretching out there for miles, you'd never find your way in here. Well, well—I must say it's a nice little smugglers' haunt!"

The motor-boats looked like toys from where the boys stood. They were very high up indeed. The strong wind almost blew their heads off their shoulders. They could see for miles and miles round the island, on every side.

"No wonder the smugglers knew when my father was coming!" said Andy. "They could sight his boat miles away! I wonder if they sighted ours, when we went to the Cliff of Birds."

"They did the second time," said Tom. "That's why they sent out that motor-boat to stop us!"

"You're right," said Andy. "My word—what a huge smuggling business this must be—all those motor-boats! I suppose they send them out to ships lying at anchor some miles away—ships that have seen this signal—and take off their goods to bring them here in safety. This is a wonderful hiding-place."

"Where do they smuggle the goods to?" said Tom. "And why do they smuggle them? To save paying duty on them, I suppose. They get them into the country this way. But how do they get them away from here! There's no road overland even from the Cliff of Birds."

"It's a puzzle," said Andy. "If only we could escape and report all this."

"Do you remember I told you about all those boxes and crates in that cave in the Cliff of Birds?" said Tom. "How do you suppose they get them there from here?"

Andy couldn't answer him. The two boys stood looking out at the magnificent view for some time, watching the motor-boats at rest, and seeing men unload the motor-boat that had just come slipping through the narrow opening.

"I bet that boat went out last night to whatever ship Bandy was signalling to with his lamp," said Andy. "I just bet that motor-boat was loaded up miles out to sea, and slipped back here whilst it was still not dawn. She just got in in time."

"They must have men who know these rocks like a book," said Tom. "I wouldn't care to chug through them!"

"I think we'd better get back to the girls," said Andy. "They'll be longing to know all we've seen. If only we could get back home!"

They turned to go down the steps. It was dark down there. But they did not like to switch on their torches now, in case Bandy was about and spotted them. So they made their way down cautiously, feeling for the steps with their feet, and taking rather a long time to get down.

"Be careful! We're getting near to that big cave-room where we took the ham and cake from," whispered Andy.

They came to the big cave. It was still lighted by the big ship's lantern, swinging from the roof. Quietly Andy slid his head in to see if Bandy was there.

He could hear him as well as see him! The little bandy-legged man was lying on one of the mattresses, flat on his back, fast asleep. His mouth was open and he was snoring loudly.

"There's no one else there," said Tom, looking round

quickly. "But he hasn't finished that tongue or the peaches, Andy. Let's get them."

"No—he might wake up," said Andy, pulling Tom back.

"He won't. He's snoring hard," said Tom. "Come on, let's get the stuff. We haven't had any breakfast!"

He and Andy stole quickly into the huge cave. They snatched up the dish of peaches and the dish of tongue. As they turned to go, Bandy gave such an enormous snore that he made Tom jump. The boy tripped over an uneven piece of rocky floor and fell headlong. The glass dish he was carrying smashed to pieces, and both Tom and Andy were covered with juice.

"Fathead!" hissed Andy, and dragged him up. They tore to the passage. But Bandy was wide awake now, and sitting up. He yelled loudly:

"What, you come back again to steal my food, Stumpy! After the lamming I gave you last night too! You greedy fellow, you pig, you. . . ."

"Run! He thought we were the fellow that he went and lammed last night!" gasped Andy. "Run! We'll hide somewhere before he catches us."

Bandy was really on the warpath this time! To think that Stumpy was taking his food again! He'd teach him! He'd catch Stumpy, and knock his stupid head against the wall. He'd . . .

The boys fled down and down. They passed the forking tunnel that led to the cave where they had twice been bolted in. They tore on down, hoping soon to get to the place where the tunnel split in two, one part going down, and the other going back to the place where they had entered the hill by way of the moving rock.

"Once we get to that forking of the tunnel we'll be all right!" panted Andy. "We can slip out of the entrance there and make our way back to the girls!"

They came to it at last and ran along it to get out into the sunshine. But when they got to the end of that passage, the big rock had been slid back into place again! There was no way out.

"Blow! How do we move it from this side to open?" wondered Andy. He pushed and pulled and shoved, but the rock would not move. There seemed to be nothing at all that the boys could find to use as a lever this time, either. The rock was fast shut.

"Somebody's been along here, found the rock entrance open and shut it," said Andy at last. "It's no good. We can't open it."

"Well, we can't go back up the tunnel to Bandy's room," said Tom. "He'd be sure to catch us sooner or later."

"Let's go to where the tunnel forks, and take the downward path this time," said Andy. "We'll see where it leads to. It might perhaps take us out another way. It's no good us staying here to be caught like rats in a trap."

So back they went once more, listening cautiously for Bandy. They took the downward way at the forking of the tunnel, and made their way along dark, musty passages, winding here and there.

"These passages must be right in the heart of the hill like the tunnel in the Cliff of Birds," said Tom. "Listen —what's that?"

It was the sound of a quarrel. The boys crept nearer to the shouts. "It's Bandy going for Stumpy again!" said Andy. "Poor Stumpy! We do seem to be getting him into trouble!"

Out of the tunnel another cave opened, rather like the one above, which was apparently Bandy's. This one, however, was smaller and not so well furnished. In it Bandy and Stumpy were quarrelling. The cave was not very well lighted, and the boys felt certain they could not be seen, as they stopped in the dark passage to peep in for a moment.

"Why—Stumpy is the hairy-legged man!" whispered Tom. "See his bare, hairy legs and enormous feet! He's the one that swung his legs above us that day—and I saw him again in the cave down at the foot of the Cliff of Birds, with the other man too."

There was a fine old fight going on in Stumpy's cave. Roaring and shouting and yelling, chasing round and dodging! The boys wished they could stop and watch, for the sight was rather comical. But they thought the chance of slipping by unnoticed was too good not to be taken, and they dodged quickly past the entrance of the cave. Neither of the men saw them.

And now the tunnel dipped very steeply indeed, and went downwards for a long way. "Into the very depths of the earth," said Tom in a hollow voice that quite startled Andy.

The walls of the rocky tunnel suddenly began to gleam in a queer way. "Phosphorescence," said Andy. "Isn't it curious, Tom? Most unearthly!"

"Let's go back," said Tom suddenly. "I don't like this at all. And I don't like that funny noise right over our heads, either."

Andy had noticed a queer noise too—boom, boom, boom! Booooooom!

"What can it be?" he wondered. "No, Tom, we can't go back now after coming all this way. We'll come out somewhere soon. We must! If only this tunnel would go upwards again. It's gone down so deep."

They went on again, between the wide gleaming walls. There was plenty of room in this passage—room for three men to walk abreast, if need be—and the roof was well above their heads.

They walked on, using their torches, and feeling very tired of the long, dark way. Andy was puzzled. Smuggler's Rock was not a big island. They could have walked right through it by now! Where were they going?

He suddenly stopped and clutched Tom's arm. Tom jumped violently. "Don't do that?" he said. "What's up?"

"Tom—I know where we are—and I know what that noise is!" said Andy, in an excited voice.

"What is it?" said Tom, looking at him, startled.

"It's the sea we can hear—above our heads!" said Andy.

"Above our heads?" said Tom, looking up as if he expected to see waves breaking over him. "What do you mean?"

"We're under the rocky floor of the sea!" said Andy, in a loud voice. "We're in an underground tunnel, right under the sea itself—and I bet I know where it leads to! It goes to the Cliff of Birds."

Tom gaped. He was so astonished that he couldn't say a word. He stared at Andy, and listened to the dull, muffled boom above him. Yes—it must be waves pounding away up there, far above their heads. Tom hoped the floor of the sea was good and strong! It wasn't nice to think of all that water away up there.

"That's why that tunnel sloped so steeply," said Andy. "It goes right under the sea. We must be a good way under by now—but I don't know how far we are from the Cliff

114

of Birds. I suppose we'll get there sooner or later. Now we know how the smugglers take their goods there—and store them in that cave you saw there! They carry them here, under the sea itself!"

"Come on," said Tom in excitement. "Come on— let's see where this leads to—quick!"

An Unexpected Find

THE two boys went eagerly forward along the strange tunnel. It was so wide that it could have taken two train-tracks. No wonder the smugglers could so easily carry goods from Smuggler's Rock to the Cliff of Birds!

Boom, boom, booooooom! The restless sea went on pounding away overhead. "I hope," said Tom, "that there isn't a leak in any of the rocks in the roof of this queer under-sea tunnel! It would be awful to think of the sea pouring in."

"Don't be silly! This tunnel must have existed for years," said Andy. "There's no reason why it should suddenly spring a leak! We're all right."

"I suppose we are, really," said Tom. "Blow! My torch is giving out!"

"Well, I've got two—mine, which I'm using, and Jill's," said Andy. "I gave you Mary's. We'll make do with just mine now, because we may need Jill's torch later on if mine gives out. Walk close to me. My word, don't these walls and roof gleam! It's a weird tunnel. It must have been used in the olden days quite a lot."

"I wonder who first found it and went along it," said Tom, stumbling over an uneven piece. "Here, shine your torch more downwards, Andy. I can't see where I'm going."

They went on for a long while. Andy tried to reckon out how long a tunnel would be that stretched between the Cliff of Birds and Smuggler's Rock. Surely they must be nearing the end of it now.

"Listen—that booming noise isn't nearly so loud," said Tom, suddenly stopping. "Andy, listen."

"You're right," said Andy. "Well, that can only mean one thing—we're out from under the sea now—maybe under the Cliff of Birds."

"You know, Andy—*I* think we shall probably come up into that cave where I saw all those boxes and crates stored," said Tom, thinking hard. "When I was there, I saw Stumpy and the fisherman with glasses disappear down a hole in the floor of the cave—and I bet that hole led down into this tunnel."

"I should think you're right," said Andy. "Come on, we'll soon see. It's nice not to hear the sea booming overhead any more. It wasn't a very pleasant sound. It made me feel a bit queer."

"Me too," said Tom. "I felt as if I was walking along some kind of unpleasant dream!"

On they went again. The passage was still very wide indeed, and grew even wider as they stumbled forward. Then Andy's torch flashed on more stores!

The tunnel had now widened into what looked like a big underground hall. It was lined with hurriedly piled cases of all kinds. Andy went over to them curiously, and shone his torch on them.

"Maybe they're brandy," he said. "I know that's smuggled in sometimes. Each case has got some sort of scribbled letters or numbers on. Look at all those green ones, too."

"Here's one half broken," said Tom. "Bring the torch over. We might be able to see what's inside."

Soon the torch was flashing on to the half-broken case. The boys pulled out handfuls of straw, packing and padding material.

Then Andy gave a long low whistle, and stood staring in astonishment. Tom looked at him impatiently.

"What is it? Do you know what's inside?"

"Yes—look here—see that shining barrel? There are guns here—and revolvers too, I expect. And ammunition in those green boxes over there! I bet I'm right. My word—this is more than smuggling."

"What is it then?" said Tom in a whisper. "I don't understand."

"Nor do I yet," said Andy. "I only know that those men are bringing in thousands of guns—and ammunition—and sending them from here somewhere else—either to sell to countries who are not allowed to have these things, or to use against our own country in some way. It's a plot of some sort—a dangerous plot too, which might mean

117

peril to our land and people in some way. My goodness me—no wonder those men sank our boat, kept us prisoner, and did all they could to prevent my father from finding us! "

Tom felt scared. "They won't hurt the two girls, will they?" he said, thinking of Jill and Mary left alone in the cave.

"I don't think so," said Andy. "What *are* we to do? What *can* we do? We ought somehow to get back and report this strange find—and we ought to get back to Jill and Mary and look after them! But how are we to do either! "

Tom sat down on a box. Things were happening a bit too fast. He looked fearfully round the great underground store-house. Guns! Guns by the thousand! Gunpowder too, perhaps. Ammunition waiting to be used in wicked ways by wicked people. He shivered.

Andy sat down beside him to think. The fisher-boy looked worried. He wished he was grown-up. Grown-ups always seemed to know the right thing to do and they could do it. But he didn't know what *was* the right or best thing, and even if he did, how could he do it?

"The thing is," he said out loud, "is it best to go back and try and get out on Smuggler's Rock, and find the girls —or is it best to go on, and make our way into the Cliff of Birds? Perhaps that would be best, because we could go up the tunnel there that leads to the waterfall, Tom, and maybe climb out of the opening there, into the daylight, and wait to see if my father comes hunting for us again. Then we could signal."

"Yes—that's a jolly good idea," said Tom. "The men couldn't possibly guess we have found the under-sea tunnel and come to the Cliff of Birds. Why, they may not even know we are not with the girls, if they don't go snooping round our cave. We could wait our chance and signal from the Cliff of Birds."

"It sounds all right," said Andy rather gloomily. "But I doubt if my father will come again to-day—he's been two days running and found nothing. Maybe they'll all be off searching other places now."

"Still, it really is the only thing we can do," said Tom, getting up. "Come on, we'll go right on now, shall we? We'd better be careful, though, because we might run up against one of the men in the Cliff of Birds."

So they left the underground hall behind them and made their way cautiously onwards again. The tunnel narrowed after a little while and became more as it had been before —a wide rocky passage, with a high roof.

It ran upwards suddenly. "I bet it's leading to that cave," whispered Tom. "Don't make a row, and shade your torch with your hand, Andy."

Moving very quietly now, the two boys went on. The passage suddenly came to a very abrupt end. A rocky wall barred their way!

"A blind end!" said Andy, feeling up and down it with his hands. "Blow! What does this mean?"

It didn't seem to mean anything except that the passage had ended. They could go no farther at all. Andy gave a huge sigh. He was exhausted now with his long stumbling walk, and it seemed the last straw that they should not be able to find a way out.

He sat down suddenly, and Tom fell beside him, his legs shaking with tiredness. "It's no good," said Andy. "I can't go back. I'm tired out. We're beaten!"

Tom felt the same. But after a short rest Andy felt more cheerful. He flashed his torch round again, and then suddenly turned it upwards, shining it above his head. He gave a cry and clutched Tom's arm.

"Look—what idiots we are! There's the way out—above our heads! A big hole in the roof, of course!"

Tom gazed up and saw a big round hole in the roof of the suddenly-ended tunnel. He gave a gasp.

"Of course, Andy! Didn't I tell you those two men disappeared down a hole in the floor of their cave? Well— that's the hole, I bet! It's got to lead somewhere, and it led down to this passage. Why didn't we flash our torch upwards before?"

Both boys immediately felt better. So much better, in fact, that they both leapt up and were prepared to go on for miles again, if need be! Andy tried to see how to climb up. But there was no sign of steps or footholds of any kind.

"What's that—twisted round something there?" whispered Tom suddenly. Andy shone his torch. He saw a rope caught round an iron staple driven into the rock. The rope was as dark as the rock, and neither of the boys had noticed it before. They had been looking for steps cut out, or for iron footholds.

"That's it—that's the way to get up and down!" whispered Andy. "We'll go up right away! I don't imagine there's anybody in the cave above, or we should see a light of some sort. I'll go first, Tom. Hold the torch for me."

Tom took the torch. His hand was trembling with excitement and relief, so the light was rather shaky! Andy untwisted the rope and took hold of it. It was firm and strong. The fisher-boy went up it like a monkey. He was used to ropes!

He found himself in the darkness. He had no idea where he was, once he had climbed up out of the hole. He looked down and saw Tom's anxious face in the light of the torch.

"Throw up the torch!" he said. "Careful, now. That's it. Now, I'll shine it down for you. Catch hold of the rope. Come on!"

Tom climbed up the rope too, and Andy gave him a helping hand at the top. They stood up and looked round by the light of their torch.

"Yes—this is the cave I told you about—the one with the stores—where the underground river rushes nearby," said Tom. "Good thing there's no one here!"

Andy flashed his torch at the piles of boxes. "Those are food-stores," he said. "See? There's a box half-unpacked, look—full of tinned food to feed all the men who help in this unlawful work. My word, whoever planned this planned it very thoroughly! I suppose this food goes to feed all the crews of those motor-boats."

"I'll show you where the underground river flows," said Tom, and dragged him behind the pile of boxes at one side of the cave. He showed him the hole beyond which the dark river rushed in its narrow tunnel. "That's where I jumped in!" said Tom.

"Well—we won't go that way," said Andy. "It's a bit too dangerous for my liking! We'll go up, not down, Tom —up that twisting tunnel you found, that leads to the waterfall opening—and we'll hope the torrent of water will be small enough to-day for us to creep out of the opening."

"And then we'll wait on the cliff and signal!" said Tom. "We'll soon be rescued! Come on, Andy—into the tunnel we go!"

Andy Gets a Real Surprise

ANDY and Tom left the store-cave behind, and went into the tunnel that led upwards. Tom was sure he knew the way. He remembered how he had first found his way into it—he had squeezed through the waterfall entrance, found himself in a big cave, gone into the next cave and found steps leading upwards . . . and from there had found his way down the twisting tunnel to the store-cave they had just left.

Yes, he knew the way all right. There was no chance of making a mistake, anyway, because as far as he remembered, there had only been the one tunnel to follow. It hadn't kept forking into two, as the tunnel had in Smuggler's Rock.

So flashing their torches in front of them, the boys began the long, tiring pull upwards. It seemed much longer to Tom than it had been before.

"Well, it's because it goes *up* this time, not down!" said Andy, who was panting too. "It must be much easier going down it than up. My, what a climb!"

After a time, Tom stopped in surprise. He shone his torch in front of him and stared, puzzled.

"Why, Andy, look—the passage splits into two here, after all—and I felt sure it didn't. I felt sure there was only the one way to follow! Blow! I can't have noticed it, when I came down!"

Andy examined the fork of the tunnel. "No—you wouldn't notice it," he said. "You'd come round that dark corner—see—and wouldn't see there was another way leading off here, because of that jutting-out rock—and you'd just go on down without noticing it. Come on."

"But, Andy, wait—I'm not at all sure which passage I came down in!" said Tom. "I might have come by either, and not noticed the other one. Oh, which one did I take?"

"Well, really—I should have thought you would have known that!" said Andy rather unfairly, for the two tunnels looked exactly alike in the darkness. Tom didn't know. He stood and stared at them both, wondering which was the right one.

"Well, it doesn't really matter," said Andy at last. "We'll take the right-hand one and hope for the best. If it doesn't lead out on the cliff, we can easily go back and take the other one."

"Yes, we could," said Tom, relieved. "Come on, then, let's take this one. It may be the right one. I have a feeling it is."

But his feeling was wrong. It was most decidedly the wrong one! It twisted and turned much more than the right one had, and Tom soon was quite certain they were wrong.

"Better go back," he said. "I'm sure this isn't right."

"Well, I wonder where it leads to then," said Andy, puzzled. "It's going upwards. Do you think it leads to the top of the Cliff—or goes to the other side of the shallow bay where we once anchored the *Andy*? It must come to an end soon, I should think. We might as well just see what happens!"

So they went on, and were soon rewarded by seeing what they thought must be daylight shining far ahead. And sure enough it was!

The passage suddenly came out from a deep cleft in the high cliff, and there, below them, was the sea, crashing over the rocks that studded that coast for miles on end.

They sniffed the fresh air in delight. After the mustiness of the tunnel, it was delicious. It was lovely, too, to feel the clean, cool wind on their faces.

They sat down on the ledge, scaring away half a dozen indignant nesting-birds. The disturbed eggs rolled round and round in a circle, but fortunately did not drop off the ledge.

"Now if we just had something to *eat*," said Tom. He put his hand into his pocket, and to his great delight found a piece of ham and a half-piece of cake. The boys shared his find together hungrily, wishing there was more.

"We are higher up than we were before, when we were on the waterfall ledge," said Andy. "I wonder where we are exactly? We're not right at the top of the Cliff. I think we've gone beyond the Cliff of Birds, and are now on a ledge the other side. Let's lean over the ledge and see if the cove we anchored in is down below us, or not. I don't think it is."

"Well, you look down," said Tom. "It's a bit too high up even for me! I shall feel giddy if I lean over the ledge at this height."

"Hold my legs and I'll go to the edge and put my head over," said Andy. He lay down flat on his tummy and worked himself to the edge of the sharp ledge. Tom laid hold of his ankles and held them firmly.

Andy looked down. Miles below, as it seemed, the sea moved silently and slowly towards the cliff. The boys were too high up to hear any sound of the sea at all. It was queer to look down and see so far below.

Andy's eyes swept the coast-line just there. It was as he had thought—they were no longer above the cove where they had once anchored the *Andy*. They must be farther round the coast.

The boy's eyes examined the shore below closely—and then he saw something that made him stare so hard that his eyes blurred and he couldn't see.

"Hold me fast, Tom, hold me," he cried. "I'm going to wriggle a bit farther forward—I must see what's exactly below us, miles down. Hold me tight!"

Tom tightened his grip of Andy's sturdy ankles, as the boy hung himself a bit farther over the ledge, the better to see what was below. He stared. He stared in silence for so long that Tom got impatient.

"What is it?" he said. "I'm tired of hanging on to you. What can you see?"

Andy couldn't believe what he saw. He shut his eyes, and then opened them again. Yes, it was still there. How very extraordinary—and how very, very marvellous!

He slid back on his tummy, and sat up, his face happy and glowing. His eyes shone so brightly that Tom was startled.

"Andy—what's up?" he said.

"Tom! Do you know what's down there—hidden in a little channel of water, in a fold of the cliff itself?" said Andy, in a voice that shook with excitement. "You'll never guess, never!"

"What?" cried Tom.

"Our boat!" yelled Andy, and beat on the rocky ledge with his hands. "OUR BOAT—the *Andy*!"

"But she's sunk," said Tom, thinking that Andy must be mad. "You know she is."

"I know she *isn't*!" said Andy. "Wouldn't I know my own boat, that I've sailed in scores of times? Those men were telling lies to us. They haven't sunk the *Andy*! They've got her down there, hidden in a fold of the rocks —oh, a very, very clever hiding-place indeed! I don't believe anyone could possibly spot her from the sea. She could only be spotted from just up here!"

"But, Andy—oh, Andy, it can't be!" said Tom, a ridiculous tear spurting out from the corner of one eye. "I was sure she was sunk! What a mercy we took the wrong passage and got up here! We wouldn't have known about her if we hadn't, would we? How simply, absolutely marvellous!"

"Want to see her?" said Andy. "Want to have a peep at our dear old boat? She hasn't got her sail up, but I knew it was her! I nearly fell over when I first spotted her. Good thing you were holding my legs, Tom!"

"Well—you hold mine jolly tightly," said Tom, and laid himself down on his tummy. Soon he was peeping over the edge of the cliff, and saw, far down below, a tiny boat tucked away in a small channel of water, hidden by a fold in the rocks.

"Is it really the *Andy*?" he said. "I wouldn't be able to tell. She looks all deck to me. But there's a red spot on her which must mean her sail is folded up there. They've put it back again."

"It's the *Andy* all right," said Andy joyfully. "I'd know her out of a million boats. What a bit of luck! She hasn't been sunk! We know where she's hidden. Now we've only got to get her, and we can sail away home!"

"Yes—but how are we going to get her?" said Tom, wriggling back. "*That* won't be easy!"

The two boys leaned against the rock at their backs and discussed what would be the best thing to do now. Plainly they must try to get down to the *Andy*. The whole difficult problem of escape would be solved if only they got her.

"We can't possibly climb down the cliff here, and get to her," said Andy. "We should fall and be dashed to pieces. It seems to me that absolutely the only thing to do is to get down to our own cove somehow—the one the underground river flows into—and climb round the rocks at the base of the cliff till we reach the *Andy*. It will take ages!"

"Oh goodness—and we've got no food," said Tom dolefully. "That doesn't seem a very good idea to me."

"Well—think of a better idea then, and we'll follow it," said Andy. But of course Tom could think of nothing else at all.

"You're right," he said at last with a sigh. "It's the only thing to do. But, Andy, let's get back to that store-cave, where the boxes of food are kept. We could open some of those tins and at least have something to eat. We can't go on too long without food. At least, I can't."

"All right," said Andy. "Anyway, Tom, I think it would be better to keep in hiding till the evening, in case anyone sees us clambering about the rocks to get to the *Andy*. Come on, we'll get down to the store-cave now and get what food we want. Then we'll take it up to the ledge by the waterfall—if we can get through the waterfall entrance—and wait there till we think it's safe to climb down and get round the rocks to find the *Andy*."

It was easier to get down to the store-cave than it had been to climb from it up to the Cliff! There was no one there. The boys hunted about and found two or three tin-openers. Good! They each put one in their pockets and then chose a few tins to take with them.

"Tongue," said Tom. "And spam. And pears and apricots and plums. That's *my* selection!"

They hunted about for sacks to put them in and found some old bags. Each boy put his selection of tins into a bag, threw it over his shoulder, and set out again to the cliff—but this time they took the other tunnel, when they came to the fork. Andy was amazed to see the caves where the torrent of water ran through, on its way to the waterfall.

"There's hardly any water pouring out to-day, thank goodness!" said Tom. "Come on, Andy—it'll be difficult wriggling along that narrow ledge to the entrance with our tins."

It was—but they managed it. And there they were at last, out on the ledge of the Cliff of Birds, and sitting down at the back of the shallow cave where Tom had left his ill-fated camera!

"Now for a meal!" said the ever-hungry Tom. "And then—a good long doze in the sun! After that—all set to find the good old *Andy*!"

Down to the *Andy*—
and What Happened There

THE boys had a very good meal up on the ledge in the sun.
They talked about the girls and wondered how they were
getting on, and if they were all right.

"At any rate, they've got food," said Tom. "I wish they
could share this spam and peaches with me. It's an awfully
good mixture."

"How you can cut yourself a bit of spam and then spear
a peach and eat it beats me!" said Andy. "I don't like
mixing up things like that. Isn't this sun delicious, Tom?
The wind has dropped a bit. I say—what shall we do when
we get the *Andy*? Go and rescue the girls first—or run
straight for home and report what we know?"

"I don't see how we *can* rescue the girls," said Tom,
spearing a bit of spam and a peach together on the end of
his knife. "We should only be seen by the men looking out
for your father's boat, and they'd capture us again. We'd
better run for home. The wind will be behind us, won't it?
So we could get back fairly quickly."

"Yes. I feel worried about the girls, though," said Andy,
lying down on his back, unable to eat any more. "I'm afraid
those men will be very angry when they find we've escaped
—if they do find it out—and they'll make things unpleasant
for Jill and Mary, perhaps."

This was a horrid thought. Andy was very fond of the
two girls, and Tom loved his twin sisters dearly. But if they

went back to Smuggler's Rock to get the girls, they might get captured themselves again, and what would be the use of that?

Andy fell asleep before he had time to worry any more about it. Tom drank the last drop of sweet juice from his tin, then lay back in the sunshine too, and shut his eyes. Both boys were really exhausted with their exertions.

They did not wake until the sun was well down in the west. Andy sat up and shook Tom.

"Tom! Wake up! It's time we climbed down and made a search for the *Andy*. We'll get down to the foot of the cliffs, and then try to make our way westwards, round the place where those rocks jut right out. We ought to come across the fold in the cliff where the *Andy* is hidden, sooner or later. The tide is going out, so the rocks will be fairly well uncovered."

Tom yawned as he sat up. He felt stiff. He did not like the thought of the long climb downwards. But it had to be faced. Andy began to climb down first, and Tom followed.

When they were at the foot of the cliff at last, Andy turned westwards, and began to clamber over the rugged rocks uncovered by the tide. They were slippery with sea-weed, but both boys were very sure-footed and hardly slipped at all.

They made their way round the point and came in sight of another stretch of wild, rocky coast. Somewhere hidden along there was the *Andy*! But where? There was no sign of her from where they stood. She was in a very clever hiding-place indeed.

"See—that's the way they brought her in," said Andy, pointing to a narrow little sea-path free of rocks. "The men must know these coasts like the palm of their hands! There are some jolly clever sailors among them."

Slowly they made their way along the rocks that skirted the cliff. looking out for some bend that would mean the sudden fold that hid the *Andy*. But it really seemed as if it was impossible to find!

Then they found it! They rounded a steep rock, as tall as a church—and saw a narrow deep-blue runway of water running into a fold of the cliff.

"This is it!" said Andy in delight. "See? Quite hidden except from above, way up the cliff there—or here where we stand looking right in. What a blessing we spotted the boat from above. We'd never have found her any other way."

They went up the little runway of water that lay quietly in a hollowed-out channel of rock. It twisted right into the fold of the cliff—and there, at the end of it, lying quietly at anchor was the *Andy*! The boys stood still and stared at her in proud delight. What a darling of a boat she was!

"And not sunk after all!" said Tom. "Poor old Andy— you were awfully miserable about that, weren't you?"

"Yes—more than I'd ever been in my life before," said Andy. "Anyway—there she is, waiting for us. Is anyone about, do you think?"

There didn't seem to be anyone at all. Not a sound was to be heard except the usual wind and sea and bird noises. No one whistled, no one shouted. It seemed quite safe to go and explore the *Andy*.

She hadn't got her sail up, but it was there on the deck. Andy saw that the oars had been put back too. Good!

The boys made their way towards the boat. She was stripped of everything, of course, for the children had taken the things from her themselves, and put them in their cave in Smuggler's Rock. Still, what did that matter? The boat herself was there, safe and sound!

They were soon on board her. Andy examined her lovingly from top to toe. Yes, she was all right. No harm had come to her at all.

It was getting rather dark. Andy looked up at the sky. "I think it wouldn't be a bad idea if we set off now," he said. "It will be dark long before we get home—but we must chance the journey, and hope we shan't strike a rock. I know the way pretty well now."

The boys thought they would row the *Andy* carefully out of the narrow little creek, and put up the sail as soon as they got out to sea. They began to make ready to pull up the anchor.

They were just about to haul it up when Andy's sharp ears caught an unusual sound. He stopped and put his hand on Tom's arm. "Listen," he said. "Can you hear anything?"

Tom listened, trying to make out something besides the wind and the sea. At first he could hear nothing. Then he did hear something.

"Yes. I can hear the sound of some regular noise," he

said, "chug, chug, chug, chug. Oh, Andy, is it one of their motor-boats somewhere near?"

"Yes," said Andy. "That's just about what it is! Oh, I hope it's not coming in here! Just as we were getting off too. The noise is louder, Tom. We'd better hide in case the motor-boat *is* coming in here! "

The boys climbed over the side of their boat and looked about for a hiding-place. There were plenty there! Rocks stuck up all over the place.

"Let's climb up a bit, just over there," said Andy, pointing. "See where I mean? There's a good rock there we can hide behind, and see everything from. Hear everything too! Come on! The engine of that motor-boat is going more slowly. I believe it's nosing its way in here this very minute."

The boys climbed quickly up to the big rock, about six feet above the *Andy*. They crouched down there, waiting. Andy suddenly clutched Tom and pointed.

"There it is! " he whispered. "See, coming in down the little creek, up to the *Andy*. Pity it's so dark now. I can hardly see who's on the motor-boat."

The motor-boat nosed its way up and came to rest beside the *Andy*. A man jumped out and called to someone else.

"It's Bandy," whispered Tom. "I think the other man is Stumpy, isn't he? The man with the hairy legs. What are they going to do?"

A lamp was lighted on the motor-boat, and another one was placed on the fishing-boat nearby. Then Bandy and Stumpy got very busy. What they were doing the boys could hardly make out, in the deepening twilight.

"They seem to be carrying things from one boat to the other," whispered Andy. "What *are* they doing? It's a puzzle, isn't it! "

To and fro went the men, carrying all kinds of things. Andy suddenly recognized something and he gave a low exclamation that quite startled Tom.

"Look! That's our little cooking stove, isn't it?" whispered Andy. "You can just see it in the light of that lamp. They are putting it into the cabin of the *Andy*."

Then both boys were silent, for the same thought had come to them both. The stove had been in their snug cave up on the rocks of Smuggler's Rock. Were all the things being put into the *Andy*, the things that had been taken

The men were carrying things from one boat to another

from that cave? And if so, what was happening to the girls? The men must have climbed up to the cave, discovered that the boys were gone and that only the girls were there—and then what had happened? Where could the girls be? They must have been turned out of the cave if all the things were taken away.

Now the two boys were really worried. They couldn't bear to think of Jill and Mary, frightened and alone, in the hands of those grim smugglers.

Everything seemed puzzling again. Why bring the things back to the *Andy*? What was the sense of it? Why not leave them where they were—and the girls too? And above all, *where* were the girls?

The two men worked hard for some time, and then, apparently, had transferred all the things they meant to, for they put out the light on the *Andy*. Both of them went back to the motor-boat, sat down and lighted cigarettes.

"Are they going to stay here all night?" whispered Tom in dismay. "We'll never get away if they do!"

"Well, we can't get off till they go, because they are blocking the way out for the *Andy* now," said Andy in a gloomy whisper. "Pity we didn't get off a few minutes sooner."

"They'd have seen us and given chase," said Tom. "It's just as well we didn't. I wish they'd go. It would be so nice to get back home with the *Andy*, everything complete in her again! If only we knew about the girls."

When they had smoked their cigarettes, the two men got up. They had had very little to say to one another, and then only commonplace remarks. Andy wondered if Bandy was still angry with Stumpy for apparently stealing his food.

"We'll go and have a word with the Chief," said Bandy, throwing his glowing cigarette end into the water. "We'll see if anyone has found those dratted boys. Good thing we've got the girls to bargain with—nice little hostages they are!"

The men climbed on to a ledge, and made their way up the creek. Andy and Tom could not see where they went, because it was now almost dark.

"Must be some entrance into the Cliff of Birds up that way," muttered Andy in Tom's ear. "I wonder who the Chief is! Perhaps that fellow with the glasses you once saw in the store-cave with Bandy, Tom. Wonder how long they're going to be? I've a good mind to take their motor-boat and chance the run home in it! I know how to drive one!"

Tom was cold with the evening wind, and with suspense. He shivered now with excitement.

"What! Take their boat, Andy?" he said. "Would you really dare?"

Who is in the Cabin?

IT was quite dark now. The sky was perfectly clear, and the stars shone out, giving so little light that in that shut-in creek there was none to see by. Only the lamp on the motor-boat gleamed out, showing the deck there.

Andy listened for the men's voices. No—there was no sound of them. They had gone—but for how long? What had to be done must be done now if they were to get away quickly.

The boys got down from their hiding-place and crept softly over the rocks to the waiting motor-boat. It was quite still on the narrow waters of the calm little creek. They climbed over the sides, and examined it.

It was whilst they were looking at it to see how to start it up that they were startled by a noise in the cabin of the boat. It was a curious noise—a kind of long-drawn-out groan!

The boys stood absolutely still, almost startled out of their wits, for they had been so certain they were alone. They listened. The groan came again.

"There's someone here—in that cabin!" whispered Andy in Tom's ear. "We'd better get out, quick! We don't want to be discovered here. Come on. Quiet now!"

The boys climbed out as quietly as they could. They made for their hiding-place again, puzzled.

"Who's in there?" whispered Tom. "He sounded as if he was ill, or hurt. Who is it?"

"Goodness knows!" said Andy. "All I know is he's a frightful nuisance, whoever he is—he's prevented us from taking the boat."

"What shall we do now?" whispered Tom. "We can't stay up here all the night!"

"Oh, those men will come back soon," said Andy. "Then maybe they'll push off, and we can get going in the *Andy*. We must wait and see."

The boys sat themselves down and prepared to wait with what patience they could. Tom shivered again. He and Andy sat as close together as possible, for warmth.

"Can you hear any more groans?" asked Tom. Andy shook his head. "No. They seem to have stopped."

But they began again a little later. Then other noises began. Someone hammered on the door of the motor-boat's cabin. Someone shook the door violently and kicked it hard! The boys listened, more startled than ever.

Then a voice they knew very well indeed came up to them, a voice muffled by the door of the cabin, but quite unmistakable!

"Let me out! Where am I? You let me out or I'll kick the place down!"

The boys felt their hearts jump, and they stared down at the motor-boat in amazement.

"It's Jill! It's Jill's voice!" said Andy, forgetting to whisper in his enormous astonishment. "But what's Jill doing there! Quick, let's go to her!"

The boys leapt down again, not caring if they fell or not, they were so eager to reach the little girl. She was going quite mad with fury in the locked cabin. She was now hitting the door with something—crash, crash, crash. Andy couldn't help smiling. He had seldom seen Jill in a temper, but he knew she had one. He wondered if Mary was there too. If so, she was very quiet.

Andy landed on the motor-boat first and ran to the cabin-door. Jill was now raining heavy blows on it, and shouting so loudly that she could not hear Andy's voice calling to her.

"Jill! Jill! Stop all that hammering so that I can unlock the door and get in! You'll hit me if you don't stop it!"

But the furious little girl went on and on, quite beside herself. Crash, smash, crash! What in the world had she got in her hand?

There was a pause at last, and Jill, plainly quite tired out, began to sob bitterly. Andy hammered on the door with his fist.

"Jill! It's me, Andy! We're going to unlock the door and come in. Don't smash at it any more!"

There was a dead silence inside the cabin. Jill evidently couldn't believe her ears! Then there was a wild cry of joy.

"Andy! Oh, Andy, darling Andy, unlock the door quick!"

Andy unlocked and unbolted the door. Jill flung herself on him and Tom, weeping for joy.

"I thought you were lost for ever!" she sobbed. "We didn't know what to make of it when you didn't come back. The men said you never would. We thought you must be drowned. Oh Andy, oh Tom, let's go home!"

"Where's Mary?" asked Tom.

"In the cabin—on that bunk there—she won't wake up," said Jill. Andy took the lamp from the deck of the motor-boat and flashed the light on to where Mary was lying in a bunk.

"What's wrong with her?" he asked, hearing her breathing very loudly indeed.

"I don't know," said Jill. "I think it must have been something those men gave us to drink that sent us off to sleep like that. I didn't drink so much as Mary did—I didn't like the taste of mine—but Mary drank all hers. And then we fell fast asleep, and didn't know what was happening. I woke up just now and felt awfully sick, and I groaned and groaned."

"Yes—we heard you," said Andy. "Poor old Jill. I expect Mary will wake up soon. My word, Jill, you nearly broke that door down! What did you hit it with?"

"That stool," said Jill. "I felt so angry when I knew those men had put us somewhere and left us. I don't know where we are, you see. We fell asleep in that cave high up in Smuggler's Rock—where the men put us all before, when Andy's father came to look for us."

"You've got a lot to tell us," said Andy, "and we've got some pretty peculiar things to tell you too. But we can't stop now to exchange news, because those men may come back at any time. We don't want all to be captured again."

"No—this is a jolly good chance to escape, the whole lot of us," said Tom. "But, Andy—we must tell them *one* thing!"

Andy knew what that was, of course! "Oh yes," he said. "Jill—the *Andy* wasn't sunk! She's close by this very boat,

136

sails and oars and everything! The man must have taken her and hidden her there. She's safe and sound. Tom and I were just about to run home in her, if we could, when Bandy and Stumpy brought this motor-boat up the creek and we had to hide."

"*Oh!*" said Jill in joy. "Andy, I'm so awfully glad. I was miserable about her, of course, but I knew you must be ten times more miserable!"

"We were almost at the top of the cliff when Andy saw her," said Tom. "He'd have fallen over with joy if I hadn't had hold of his ankles!"

Andy suddenly remembered that Bandy and Stumpy might come back at any moment. "Look here—we mustn't chatter like this," he said. "We must make up our minds what we are going to do. Tom and I were thinking of running for home in this motor-boat, as we can't get at the *Andy*. This boat is blocking up the way, and we can't get the *Andy* out."

"Well, let's go, then!" said Jill eagerly. "It's awfully dark, though. I don't know how you'll see your way, Andy."

A deep groan from the cabin bunk made them jump. It was Mary, waking up after her long sleep, feeling sick. Jill went to her.

"It's all right, Mary. You'll soon feel all right."

Mary, half-asleep still, and feeling very sick, groaned again.

"Let's get her up into the open air," said Andy. "She'll feel better then. She's awfully pale."

The two boys helped the poor little girl out of her bunk. Still feeling very sick she went on deck, and was glad to feel the cool wind on her face. She soon stopped groaning.

"I feel a bit better," she said feebly. "Tom, Andy—how is it you're here? Where are we?"

"Tell you all about it soon," said Andy. "No time now. We'll start up this motor-boat and get going as soon as we can. Jill and Tom can tell you everything as we go."

He went to start up the engine. But no matter how he tried, the engine wouldn't start up. It made a humming noise, but nothing more happened. Andy could have cried!

"What's up? Can't you get her going?" said Tom. "Here —let *me* have a try!"

But although they all had a try, nobody could start up

the motor of the boat. Why, they didn't know. It was most aggravating—especially as they couldn't possibly go on the *Andy*, because the motor-boat was in the way!

"Look out—there's someone coming," said Tom, suddenly. "See the light of their cigarettes up there?"

The four children stared up the narrow creek. Yes, there was certainly someone coming—two people, for there was the glow from the ends of two cigarettes. It must be Bandy and Stumpy coming back. Blow!

"Skip out of the boat quickly!" whispered Andy, giving Jill a helping hand. "Shut the cabin-door, Tom, and lock it. The men may slip off without looking in and seeing that the girls aren't there. If they do go, we can all get away in the *Andy*. Hurry!"

Tom locked and bolted the door of the cabin. Then he joined the others on the ledge and they all crept behind a rock, wishing their hearts were not beating so loudly.

Bandy and Stumpy came along, smoking. They clambered on board their boat. The children hardly dared to breathe. Would they be able to start up the engine, and go? How they hoped and prayed that they would hear the roar of the engine, and know that it would soon take the boat safely away from them. Then into the *Andy* they would climb, and away they would go!

Stumpy's voice came to them. "Those girls all right, do you think, Bandy? They ought to have waked up by now. That sleeping-draught you gave them wasn't too strong, was it? Funny they haven't come round from it yet."

"Aw—let them alone," came Bandy's hoarse voice. "What does it matter if I gave it to them strong? Keep them quiet! We'll have to carry them from the cabin to their boat, if they're not awake, that's all. We'll dump them down into their boat's cabin, and lock them in safely. No one will ever know where they are—and if those two boys ever get back home and split on us, well, we'll have those two girls as hostages—our safety against theirs! A nice bit of work."

"Well, I'll get one of the girls now," said Stumpy, and he unlocked the cabin-door. "Here, hand me the lamp." There was a moment's silence as he took the lamp and swung its light into the cabin. Then he suddenly gave a loud cry.

"What's this! There's nobody here! Those two girls have *gone*!"

Andy Has a Fine Idea

BANDY and Stumpy were filled with the utmost amazement to find their two prisoners gone. The children heard their astonished remarks as they searched the little cabin.

"But the door was still locked and bolted! How *could* they have gone?"

"Kids can't walk through locked doors—and there's no window they could open."

"We left them fast asleep here. I looked in at them before we went—*and* locked and bolted the door afterwards! "

"I know. I saw you. I'll swear to that."

"Then what's happened to them? Here's the cabin, just as it was when we left it—locked *and* bolted—and we come back to find it still locked *and* bolted—and the kids gone. I don't like it."

"Look here—do you suppose anyone came along and let them out—and locked and bolted the door again?" suddenly said Bandy's hoarse voice. There was a pause before Stumpy answered.

"It's possible—but who's about here in the middle of the night—here, in this lonely place? Nobody! It's a queer thing! Shall we go and tell the Chief?"

"Not me! " said Bandy at once. "What do you think he'd say to us if he knew his two precious prisoners were gone—his only means of bargaining, if his little game gets reported! No, Stumpy—we've got to find those girls somehow. They can't be far away. Now can they?"

"No. You're right there," said Stumpy. "Their own fishing-boat is still here—and they're not likely to swim down this creek, or to climb the cliff here either, unless they want to break their necks. They must be hereabouts."

"Search the motor-boat first," said Bandy. "And then the fishing-boat yonder. It's a pity we didn't carry them there, as we were told to do, dump them down in the cabin and bolt the hatch over them."

"Well, if they could get out of a locked and bolted door here, they could have got out of a bolted cabin in their own boat," said Stumpy. "Come on—they're not on our boat. Let's take our torches and look around all these rocks."

The children began to tremble. Bandy and Stumpy were two fierce men, and angry ones now too. It would not be pleasant to be found by them. Andy frowned. What could he do to distract the men from hunting round the rocks?

An idea came to him. He bent down and groped about for a stone or piece of rock. He found one and stood up again. He tried to make out where the *Andy* was, and then, taking aim, he flung the rock as hard as he could in her direction. It fell on the deck of the fishing-boat with a loud crash, that echoed up and down the little creek.

Tom, Jill and Mary jumped violently. They had not known what Andy was going to do. But Bandy and Stumpy jumped even more violently!

"Gosh—did you hear that?" said Bandy's voice. "What was it? It sounded as if it came from the fishing-boat yonder. That's where they are! Come on, quick. We'll get them, the tiresome little brats!"

Forgetting all about searching the rocks, the two men hurried to where the *Andy* floated. They climbed on deck —and after them climbed Andy, as soft-footed as a cat. A wild plan was in his head. He didn't know if he could carry it out or not—but it was worth trying!

The men flashed their torches about the boat and lifted up the folded sail. Nobody there, of course.

"They'll be down in the cabin!" said Bandy. "Come on —we'll see. And won't I shake the little varmints when I get hold of them!"

He opened the hatch and leapt down into the little cabin. Stumpy stood above it, looking down. And suddenly something happened to him that gave him the shock of his life!

Something hurled itself at his back and sent him right off

his balance! He gave a shout of terror, and then fell head-long down the open hatch into the little cabin below. He fell right on top of the equally startled Bandy, knocking him over, so that he fell and struck his head hard against the wooden table.

His torch flew from his hand and crashed, its light going out. The little cabin was in darkness. Bandy, quite sure that some unexpected enemy had fallen upon him to kill him, began to fight like a madman.

He struck out at the horrified Stumpy, who tried in vain to stop him. Bandy was quite beside himself with anger and panic, and his great fists hammered Stumpy unmercifully, so that, in self-defence, Stumpy had to hammer back! The two men rolled over and over, pummelling each other, yelling and shouting for all they were worth!

It was pitch-black in the little cabin. Andy flashed his torch down just once, and grinned with delight to see the two rogues going for each other. Let them get on with it, by all means!

The boy slammed down the hatch, and bolted it. The noise startled the two men, and they stopped fighting. It also startled the three hidden children and they jumped. "What was that?" whispered Jill. "I wish I could see what's happening!"

A cheerful voice came over to them through the darkness. "You all right, Tom, and the girls?"

"Yes, Andy! But what was all the yelling and smashing, and that last big slam?" called back Tom, glad to hear Andy's voice again. He had had no idea why Andy had left them, nor what he was doing.

"Oh, Bandy got down into the cabin, and I shoved Stumpy in to keep him company," said Andy, still more cheerfully. "I don't think Bandy welcomed Stumpy much, because they've been fighting like wild cats! The slam you heard was the hatch closing down. It's well and truly bolted too!"

There were squeals from the two girls and a loud shout from Tom.

"Andy! You've got them prisoner! Good work, Andy, good work!"

Soon the four were on the fishing-boat, and Andy told them proudly once more how he had made the two men prisoner. It seemed too good to be true! Bandy and

Stumpy, who now knew they had been fighting each other, were doing their best to bang open the hatch.

"It's no good!" Andy yelled down to them gleefully. "It's too hefty to smash open, and you should see the bolts! Make as much noise as you like, though, so long as you can't get out."

"Are they really caught?" asked Mary, sitting down on the deck, feeling suddenly sick again. "Oh dear—all this has made me feel bad again!"

"You'll soon be all right, Mary," said Jill. "I feel quite better now. Golly, Andy, that was a good trick of yours! What are we going to do next?"

"Well, I don't somehow think anyone will be along this way to-night, so we can let those two fellows shout all they want to!" said Andy. "When dawn comes we'll set free the motor-boat, and somehow get her down the creek and out of the way of the *Andy*. Then we'll take the *Andy* and run for home."

"With Bandy and Stumpy?" asked Tom, his eyes wide with excitement.

"Well, they'll have to come too, whether they want to or not," said Andy, with a grin. "Two nice little prisoners, who will have to explain quite a lot of things to quite a lot of people very soon."

"I'll be awfully glad to get home safely," said Jill.

"So will we all," said Andy. "I vote we have a rest till dawn. We can't mess about with the motor-boat whilst it's dark."

"Oh, Andy—we've slept for ages!" said Jill. "Can't we talk? I want to know all about your adventures—and tell you what happened to us too."

"Well, fire away," said Andy. "Tom and I have had a good sleep to-day too. We'll all talk. Let's get back to the motor-boat and talk in the cabin there. It's cold here. Bandy and Stumpy have got all the rugs down in our little cabin!"

The four of them went to the motor-boat and curled themselves up in the two bunks there. They lighted the lamp too, and soon it looked quite cosy.

"Did anything much happen after we had gone?" asked Andy.

"Well, Mary and I didn't hear you leave the cave when

you went to follow the trail of shells," said Jill. "We didn't wake up till morning. We remembered where you had gone, of course, and we hoped you wouldn't be too long. We had breakfast, and then we squeezed out of the cave to wait for you."

"You didn't come, and you didn't come," said Mary. "So we thought we would follow the trail of shells ourselves, and see if we could find you! We followed them and came to where they stopped. . . ."

"I bet you didn't know where to go next!" interrupted Tom.

"We didn't," said Jill. "We couldn't imagine why the shells ended at a blank wall of rock. And then suddenly the rock opened!"

"Golly!" said Tom. "That must have scared you!"

"It did," said Jill. "It scared us terribly. We ran away —but that bandy-legged man tracked us back to our cave and yelled to us to come out."

"We had to come out in the end," said Mary, "because he threatened to smoke us out again. He thought you two boys were in there and he yelled and yelled to you to come out too. When you didn't, he crawled in—and found the cave empty!"

"What did he do then?" asked Andy, with great interest.

"He raved at us, and tried to make us say where you were," said Mary. "He was horrid. Then he hunted about all over the place and still couldn't find you. Then some other men came, and they had a sort of meeting. We couldn't hear what they said."

"They sent Bandy into our cave and he brought out everything," said Jill. "Then we were taken, blindfolded as before, back to that high-up cave in Smuggler's Rock —the one we were all put in before. We didn't have any food or drink for ages, and then Bandy came with some."

"And we think that what we drank must have had sleeping-medicine in it," said Mary, "because when we had drunk it, we simply couldn't keep our eyes open!"

"Yes. They must have given you sleeping-draughts," said Andy. "Beasts! Then they meant to bring you here and lock you into the *Andy*, keeping you as hostages in case Tom and I had escaped, and could report the whole affair to someone. What a bit of luck we happened to be here too!"

143

"Yes! Now tell us how *you* came to be here!" begged Jill. "Go on, Andy, tell every single thing."

So Andy and Tom told their tale too—and when they had finished, the dawn was coming up, and it was time to get to work again. With luck they should be home that day —and what a surprising lot of news they had for the grown-ups so anxiously looking for them!

Running for Home

AND now the four children began to be very busy indeed! The daylight filtered into the narrow, hidden creek and gave them just enough light to see by. The boys clambered on board the motor-boat, and tried once more to start up the engine. But for some reason or other again they could not get the boat to go.

"Let's untie her and give her a jolly good push!" said Andy. "She'll perhaps float away then, and give us room to get out the *Andy*."

So they untied the rope that held the motor-boat moored to a post-like rock. Then, all together, the children shoved and pushed. The boat slid away from the ledge they stood on and floated away down the creek.

"She's going!" cried Jill. "She's going down to the sea all by herself!"

"Now she's stuck," said Andy, as the boat seemed to get herself wedged against a rock. "I'll get an oar from the *Andy*, and climb into the motor-boat, and push her along by the oar."

Tom fetched him an oar from the *Andy*. Andy ran down the ledge, jumped to a rock, and from there to the deck of the motor-boat. He shoved the oar against the rock and pushed the boat out of her corner. She bobbed there, not seeming to know which way to go. Andy shoved with the oar again.

"Mind you don't break it!" yelled Tom, seeing the oar-blade bending a little. "Oh—there she goes, down the creek. Come on out, Andy, or you'll go with her!"

But Andy did not get out of the motor-boat till she was right out of the little channel. Then, when she was safely bobbing about in a patch of water outside, he clambered over the side, slithered down to a rock that was under water, and began to wade back to the rocky ledge that ran beside the creek. An enormous wave nearly sent him flying, but he managed to keep his balance.

He went back to the others, grinning. "Well, the motor-boat's out of our way all right!" he said. "That's good. Now to get the *Andy* out. We'll have to use the oars again. We'll put up the sail when we get the wind."

A great noise began again down in the cabin of the *Andy*. Bandy and Stumpy evidently knew that something was up! How they crashed and banged against the bolted hatch. But it was good and strong, and they couldn't make it budge.

"Make all the noise you like!" Andy called to the men cheerfully. "We don't mind! By the way, your motor-boat's been turned loose. I hope it won't smash to pieces on the rocks. There's a pretty good tide running, with this strong wind!"

All kinds of terrible threats came up from the cabin, but the children only laughed at them. They were feeling very happy now. They had the *Andy* back, they were all together again, they had two fine prisoners and a wonderful secret—and they were going to run home before the wind. Hurrah!

Tom, of course, wanted to finish the rest of the food in the tins that he and Andy had brought down the cliff. Andy looked at his watch, and decided they might have ten minutes for a meal. It was a very merry meal. Jill and Mary were hungry, for both girls felt perfectly all right again by now.

Then they set off. The boys worked away with the oars, getting the *Andy* carefully down the little creek of water. Big waves splashed up it now, but they managed very cleverly. The boat gradually went down the little channel, and was at last bobbing on the open sea.

"We have to follow that sea-path there between the rocks," said Andy. "Then we round the point and find ourselves opposite the shallow bay where we anchored the *Andy* before. Then we turn into the channel of water between the two long ridges of rock and run for home!"

The boat bobbed violently on the surging water. The tide was running very high indeed. The wind whipped by them, sending their hair straight up.

"Tom, take the oars and keep her off the rocks there," said Andy. "I'll put up the sail. Jill, take the tiller for a minute. That's right. Keep her headed the way she is."

Andy was just about to put up the sail when he heard a cry from Mary. "Oh look—the motor-boat is going on the rocks! Look at her!"

The children looked. Mary was right. The motor-boat was indeed on the rocks! With no one to guide her or control her she was quite at the mercy of the waves, and they had taken her right on to the wicked rocks that dotted the sea just there.

There was a smashing, grinding noise. The children's faces grew grave and solemn. It wasn't nice to see a boat smashed to pieces like that.

"Don't let's watch any more," said Tom. "It's awful to see the waves smashing it up—poor thing, it's on its side now—and look at that great hole there! When next it's swept off the rocks, it will fill with water and sink."

"One less boat for the smugglers," said Andy, and put up the red sail deftly.

The wind filled it gleefully, and the sail flapped eagerly. Andy slid down to the seat by the tiller and took it from Jill. "Put the oars in, Tom," he said. "We're all right now. Off we go with the wind!"

It was glorious to feel the little boat leaping along. "If she could sing, she would!" said Mary. "Even as it is I sometimes think her sail flaps out a kind of song!"

There came a noise from below. The children listened, trying to make out the voice against the sound of wind and waves.

"It's only Bandy saying that they feel sick down there and want some fresh air," said Tom, with a grin.

Jill put her mouth to the crack of the hatch and called down. "You made me and Mary feel sick with your horrid sleeping-medicine. It's your turn now! You won't come up here!"

"I should think not!" said Andy, and swung the tiller round as the boat entered the channel between the long, wicked rows of sharp black rocks. "Do they really think

The boat was dashed against the rocks

we'd let them come up here—to overpower us, and whisk us back to Smuggler's Rock? What a hope! "

Plainly Bandy and Stumpy didn't feel there was much hope for it, for they said no more. The children forgot about them as they raced along. They revelled in the speed of their boat, and loved the way she seemed to gallop over the white-topped waves. Andy looked the picture of happiness as he sat at the tiller, his brown face glowing and his deep-blue eyes reflecting the sea.

"Dear old Andy!" thought Jill, looking at him. "He's got back his boat, and he's happy again. It's true that it's our boat too—but he's the real skipper!"

For a long time the boat swept on over the waves, and they made very good time indeed. "We'll be home about eleven, at this rate!" shouted Andy, the wind whipping his words away as he called them out.

They swept into their home-waters just after eleven, the red sail making a bright speck on the blue waters. The children eyed the shore eagerly. Would their mother be there? Would Andy's father be there? Of course not— because they didn't know the children were coming home at that very moment!

But they *were* there, all the same! Someone had sighted the *Andy* as she turned into the harbour and the word was sent round at once. "The *Andy* is back! There she is! The *Andy* is come home again! Let's hope the children are safe and sound!"

The children's mother was fetched at once and ran down to the jetty, her face bright with hope. She had been very unhappy the last few days. Andy's father stood there too, his blue eyes watching the incoming boat. Then a shout went up.

"They're all on board, the whole four of them. They're safe! Thank God for that!"

Andy's father turned to the children's mother. "They're safe, ma'am," he said, his eyes bright with joy. "I knew they'd be all right with my Andy. Look at them waving to us. They're all right, ma'am, they're all right!"

Many willing hands made the *Andy* safe as she stopped beside the jetty. The children leapt off and ran to their mother. Andy got a hug from his father, and then he pointed back to the boat.

"We've two prisoners there, Dad. Look out for them.

they're pretty dangerous fellows. We've got them bolted down."

Everyone gaped. Andy's father rapped out a few questions and Andy answered breathlessly. Then three of the listening fishermen, stalwart, sturdy fellows, started grimly towards the *Andy*. They opened the hatch—and up came Bandy and Stumpy, looking very green indeed. They were grasped by rough, strong hands and jerked off the *Andy's* deck to the jetty.

"It's a case for the police, Dad," said Andy. "There's something very queer going on in the Cliff of Birds and Smuggler's Rock. We found cases upon cases of guns and ammunition."

The fishermen whistled and looked at one another. One of them went off to fetch the local policeman. It was all very exciting indeed!

"I'm jolly hungry," said Tom. The girls laughed. It was so like Tom to say that, in the middle of all the excitement. His mother put her arm round them.

"Come along and have a good meal," she said. "I'm so happy to have you back. You've no idea how worried I've been. Andy's father and uncle, and many of the other fishermen all went out hunting for you—and there wasn't a trace of you to be found! I'm longing to hear every single thing."

Andy's father and Andy went with them. Bandy and Stumpy were left in charge of the fishermen until the policeman came. Tom wondered what his mother had got for their meal. He felt he really could enjoy one now that all worry and trouble were ended!

Whilst Andy and the others were sitting down to a noisy and exciting meal, many things were happening. The policeman decided that all these curious affairs that the children had reported were quite beyond him, and he had rung up the superintendent in the next big town.

The superintendent, listening carefully, had been filled with amazement. Yes, certainly this was a very big affair indeed. He telephoned in his turn to headquarters and soon dozens of telegraph wires were humming with news and instructions.

Bandy and Stumpy were safely in prison, and, fearful of their own skins, they gave away all the secrets of their Chief. The children knew nothing of this, but laughed and

150

chattered as they told their mother that afternoon all that had happened. They had quite forgotten how afraid they had been, and how worried.

"When things end well, nothing seems to matter," said Tom. "I do wonder what will happen to all those smugglers, Mother!"

The End of It All

THAT evening, when the children had talked themselves out, and really thought they had nothing more to say, a very large and shining car drove up to the cottage.

Out of it stepped a neat and well-dressed little man, whose sharp clever eyes looked in turn at each of the four children.

"You don't know who I am," he said, "but I am someone in charge of very high-up affairs, and I want to ask you a few questions. My name is Colonel Knox. I've heard most of your story from Andy's father. Now, can you tell me this: Did any of you ever see the man that Bandy and Stump call the Chief?"

"Well—I did see a man once in the store-cave with Stumpy, a man wearing glasses, but dressed like a fisherman," said Tom. "I don't know if he was the Chief though."

"No. That wasn't the Chief," said the sharp-eyed man. "Stumpy has told us who that man was. We are hoping to get him to-morrow, with all the others."

"What are you going to do?" asked Tom, with great interest.

"We're going to round up all the smugglers and their boats," said Colonel Knox. "We're combing out all the passages and tunnels and caves. We're opening every case and box and crate. We shall cross-examine every man we get—and we shall set that great lamp burning you told us of, and watch for the ships that answer the signal. We shall get them too!"

"Why did they smuggle those guns and things in!" said Jill.

"There is a country that is not allowed to import fire-arms of any kind," said the Colonel. "Those arms you found were made in a distant land, and have been smuggled here to take across to this other country, where they are forbidden. As you can imagine, very high prices are paid for these forbidden fire-arms. Men in our country, I regret to say, have been acting as a go-between—that is, they smuggle the arms here, and, for a price, take them to the buyers. They make a very pretty fortune out of it."

"Oh," said the children, wide-eyed and astonished. Andy considered a moment.

"And the man you'd really like to get hold of is the one they call the Chief?" he said. Colonel Knox nodded.

"Yes. All the other fellows merely obey orders. He's the Big Brain behind it all. We've suspected this affair for a long time, but we couldn't find out how the forbidden goods were brought here, or where, nor did we know who the brain behind it was."

"And if you don't get him, he'll probably start off again somewhere else?" said Tom. "Well, I wish we could tell you who he is. Don't Bandy and Stumpy know?"

"No—all they know is that he is a tall fellow, who always wears a mask when visiting them," said Colonel Knox. "And they *think* he lives in the nearest big town, so that he can get to the Cliff of Birds without too great a loss of time, when he needs to. But as there are about fifty thousand people living in that town, it's like looking for a needle in a haystack!"

"Yes. I see," said Andy. "I do hope you get him, Colonel Knox. I say, wasn't it a bit of luck we stumbled on their haunt? It was quite an accident."

"A very happy accident for us!" said the Colonel. "We don't want our country mixed up in any affair of this sort. It was a clever idea—to have a hide-out of motor-boats in such a hidden cove—and a lamp to signal out to sea, from a place that no one else ever saw at night—and to use the tunnels and caves as store-houses."

"How did the Chief get the goods out of the Cliff of Birds and Smuggler's Rock?" asked Andy, puzzled.

"We're not quite sure yet," said Colonel Knox. "But we think there is another way out of the Cliff of Birds, leading to a flat piece of ground at the back—a good place for aeroplanes to land. It is likely that the Chief took off loads of fire-arms in his 'planes."

"My word!" said Tom. "What a dangerous plot we found! I wonder the men didn't guard us more carefully than they did!"

"Ah—they didn't know what wily birds you were!" said the Colonel, with a laugh. "But they quite meant to use the two girls as hostages, if you got home and reported their doings. That would have been very unpleasant for Jill and Mary—and I'm afraid we would have had to let the miscreants free rather than risk anything happening to the girls."

"It's a good thing we captured Bandy and Stumpy," said Andy.

"A very good thing," said Colonel Knox. "We got out of them a tremendous amount of valuable information. Enough to capture all the rest of the gang, and round up their hiding-places, and stop all their plans. It's just the Chief we can't seem to lay our hands on."

"It's a pity we never saw him," said Tom.

"A great pity," agreed Colonel Knox. "Well, I'm proud to have met you children—you're a fine brave adventurous four! I must go now—but I want you to come over to the big town where I live, and have lunch with me to-morrow for a treat. Will you do that?"

"Oh, *yes!*" cried the four.

"But how can we get there?" asked Jill. "There is only one train."

"I'll send my car for you," said Colonel Knox, and got up to go. The children took him to his sleek black car. They liked him very much.

"He's clever and kind and goes straight to the point in everything," said Tom. "I only wish we could tell him who the Chief of the smugglers is. But we can't."

The next day the car was sent to fetch the four children. They climbed into it proudly, and were soon whisked away to the nearest big town. They stopped at the grandest hotel in the place, and were met in style by Colonel Knox at the door.

They felt most important walking in with him—and when

154

Tom read the menu for the lunch he looked at his host in awe.

"Can we have all these things?" he said. "Oh, it will be the best meal we've ever had. Look, it says 'Mixed ice-creams' at the bottom. Can we have vanilla, strawberry and chocolate all mixed?"

"Yes—and coffee ice-cream as well, I believe," said Colonel Knox, laughing. "Well, sit down. Now, who wants ginger-beer to drink, and who wants lemonade, or orange?"

Soon the children were in the middle of a most glorious meal. Tom looked blissfully happy. He thought this was a wonderful reward for all the adventures they had been through.

When he was in the middle of his mixed ice-cream, he looked up and saw a man seating himself at a nearby table. He was a tall, burly fellow, with deep-set eyes and black wavy hair. He nodded to Colonel Knox.

"Who's that?" asked Tom in a low voice. The Colonel looked surprised.

"Oh—just one of the inhabitants of this town," he said. "One of our very richest, though you wouldn't think it to look at him."

Tom was staring at the man curiously. He certainly didn't look rich, for he wore his clothes carelessly and the sleeve of his coat wanted mending. His red shirt was open at the neck, and lacked a button half-way down.

Tom suddenly went as red as a beetroot with excitement. He began to burrow deep into first one pocket and then another. "Whatever's the matter?" said Andy. "Why do you look like that, Tom?"

Tom brought something out from his pocket. He pushed it across to Colonel Knox, who looked at it in the greatest surprise, thinking that Tom had suddenly gone mad.

"Sir," said Tom in a whisper, "I found that red pearl button in a cave in the Cliff of Birds. It must have belonged to one of the men there, though I never saw one with a red shirt on. But look at that man over there. He's got on a red shirt—and it has red pearl buttons exactly like this —and one is missing!"

Colonel Knox's eyes flashed from Tom's button to the man's shirt. He slipped the button into his pocket.

"Say no more now," he commanded. "Don't even look at the fellow. Understand?"

There was something in those commanding tones that made the children feel a little frightened. They obeyed, eating their ices, and keeping their eyes carefully away from the man at the other table. Colonel Knox scribbled a note on a piece of paper, beckoned to a waiter and told him to deliver it somewhere. Then the Colonel became his own charming, joking self again, and apparently took no notice at all of the man in the red shirt nearby.

"I'll let you know if your button has solved our problem," he said to Tom, when the man got up and went. "It may have! It may have! He's the one man we never even suspected. Good for you, Tom! My word, this is a great affair, and no mistake!"

So it was! Before long the whole of the motor-boats in the cove had been taken, all the crews too, and every smuggler found in the caves. The smuggled goods had been confiscated, ships that helped in the smuggling were captured, and the whole plot exposed.

And the man in the red shirt was the leader, the Chief of the whole gang! It was too good to be true that Tom should have found the button that led to his capture. Colonel Knox was very pleased about it indeed.

"You shall certainly have a fine new camera for your help with the button!" he said to Tom. "Without you we should never have known who the Chief was—no one even suspected him! He ran the whole business very cleverly indeed, and not even the men themselves ever saw him face to face. He has made a fortune out of his smuggling—but he won't make any more money for many, many years to come!"

"What a lot has happened in a week or so!" said Jill, as they all sat on the jetty that night, waiting for the fishing-boat to come back with Andy and his father. "Look, there she goes! Leading all the rest of the boats as usual. Ahoy, Andy, ahoy! We're waiting for you!"

Their mother came up to see the fishing-boats come in. As Andy stepped off on to the jetty, Tom turned eagerly to his mother.

"Mother! Can we go out with Andy in his boat next week—when he has a day off? I know a lovely place I'd like to go to."

"Certainly *not*!" said his mother. "What, lose you again

156

for days on end, and not know where you are! My dears, I shall never, never let you go out alone with Andy again!"

All the same, I expect she will. After all, they are the Adventurous Four, and there may be plenty more adventures waiting for them yet!

From Alfred Hitchcock,

Master of Mystery and Suspense—

A thrilling series of detection and adventure. Meet The Three Investigators – Jupiter Jones, Peter Crenshaw and Bob Andrews. Their motto, "We Investigate Anything", leads the boys into some extraordinary situations – even Jupiter's formidable brain-power is sometimes stumped by the bizarre crimes and weird villains they encounter. But with the occasional piece of advice from The Master himself, The Three Investigators solve a whole lot of sensational mysteries.

The Secret of Terror Castle
The Mystery of the Stuttering Parrot
The Mystery of the Whispering Mummy
The Mystery of the Green Ghost
The Mystery of the Vanishing Treasure
The Secret of Skeleton Island
The Mystery of the Fiery Eye
The Mystery of the Silver Spider
The Mystery of the Screaming Clock
The Mystery of the Moaning Cave
The Mystery of the Talking Skull
The Secret of the Crooked Cat
The Mystery of the Coughing Dragon
The Mystery of the Laughing Shadow
The Mystery of the Flaming Footprints
The Mystery of the Nervous Lion
The Mystery of the Singing Serpent
The Mystery of the Shrinking House
The Secret of Phantom Lake

Armada